RANSOM FOR A RIVER DOLPHIN

Sarita Kendall is a journalist and lives in Bogota. She covers Colombia and Ecuador for the *Financial Times*, and her first novel for children, *The Bell Reef*, is set in Colombia. She has spent a lot of time in the Amazon, gathering material for this latest book; every incident in the book derives from something that she saw, or heard tell of, there. She was born in Brazil, and has spent most of her life in South America, although she went to university in England.

SARITA KENDALL

RANSOM FOR A RIVER DOLPHIN

For my parents, who started me on my travels

First published 1992 by
Pan Macmillan Children's Books
A division of Pan Macmillan Limited
Cavaye Place London SW10 9PG
Associated companies throughout the world

ISBN 0 330 32439 X

A CIP catalogue record for this book is available from
the British Library

Typeset by Macmillan Production Limited
Printed by Clays Limited, St Ives plc

CONTENTS

Author's Note

For people who live along the River Amazon and its tributaries, dolphins are magical animals. They can slip out of the water on to the land, changing from dolphins into human beings, and they have their own underworld, with streets and houses. Magical creatures can be dangerous – or they can bring good luck: the dolphin that kidnaps a young woman washing clothes by the river may save a child who falls from a canoe.

The Amazon Basin is the only place where there are pink dolphins – and some of them are an extraordinary, dazzling pink. However, most river dolphins (*Inia geoffrensis*) are grey, or grey and pink; they have unusually big flippers and rarely jump out of the water. A smaller dolphin (*Sotalia fluviatilis*) also lives in the Amazon rivers, and is more like those that leap in the oceans.

The river world is changing as farmers move in and cut down the rainforest, as hydroelectric dams are built, chemicals washed into the water and long nets spread to catch fish. All this threatens the dolphins. But many people living in the Amazon – especially the Indians – believe that killing dolphins can bring disaster, and this belief has helped to protect the river dolphin.

The dolphin

The dolphin wove his way among the tree-trunks, swimming upside-down in the coffee-coloured water. Large flippers steered the great pink body through a maze of drowned bushes. The head swung from side to side as the dolphin scanned the muddy bottom, sending out streams of rapid clicking noises and turning the echoes into a sound picture. Every leaf and root, and all the creatures busy at the lake's edge, were clear to the dolphin, even though his eyes scarcely saw through the murk.

The long snout snatched a fish feeding on the fruit and seeds that plopped into the water from overhanging branches. The dolphin rolled and released a little air from his blow-hole, then rose to breathe.

1

Omar was ready, crouching silently in the prow of the canoe, a spear poised high in his right hand. He concentrated on the air bubbles: but his arm relaxed suddenly when the dolphin's bulbous forehead appeared. The dolphin breathed out, sighing. Omar saw a brown streak along the ridged pink back before it slid underwater, leaving a circle of ripples.

The old man stowed his spear and sat still, gazing into the trees. Ramiro, besieged by biting insects in the stern, sensed his father's dismay – he had so nearly harmed the animal.

"My eyes are going, I can't tell a fish's bubbles from a dolphin's," admitted Omar at last. "There are white hairs on my head, Ramiro. But we've caught enough fish for today."

Swinging their paddles evenly, they emerged from the deep shadow of the tangled, flooded forest into the yellow evening light. The presence of the dolphin, right under the canoe, had disturbed Omar as much as his failing eyesight. Despite the lingering heat, he shivered.

Behind the canoe, a pink head flashed briefly on the surface.

A message

"Can't hear a word," shouted the operator, fiddling with the knobs on the radio. "Louder – WHO DO YOU WANT TO SPEAK TO? Over."

The buzzing, beeping and crackling started again, with a faint, high voice breaking through every few seconds. Carmenza swung her leg to and fro, knocking blue paint off the door-frame and wondering how anyone could understand the racket coming over the radio. Yet, apart from the time she had told Mrs Rodriguez that her son had been sent to jail when he'd really joined the army, the operator seemed to get things right. Carmenza knew, because she delivered the messages and listened in to the conversations.

"It's for that old gnome Omar," said the operator. "He's to be here for a call tomorrow at three. Well, that's your last errand, I'm finished for this afternoon." She switched off the radio, tucked her orange blouse into her belt, and padlocked the door, hoping there wouldn't be any last-minute callers to force her back into the sweltering radio room.

Carmenza leaped down the four wooden steps with practised skill and had begun to run before she realised there was no hurry. Then she started to run again anyway – it made her job seem more important. People noticed her tearing along and called out to attract her attention, as if, by doing so, they too could share in the news from the outside world.

"Going to the mayor's office?" asked a woman taking in her washing. "He's down by the water fixing his out-board."

Carmenza answered with a negative toss of her head, and, puffing exaggeratedly, sped around the corner. Now she was in sight of her own house, and she glanced across to make sure her mother wasn't nearby to nag her about behaving in a more lady-like way. If being a teenager meant you should walk sedately and worry about the number of bananas you scoffed, Carmenza wasn't looking forward to becoming one.

Ahead, the path rose steeply, zigzagging among haphazardly built wooden houses with mosquito netting nailed over the windows. Pink and red flowering bushes gave off rich scents, and fruit trees shaded the yards. Carmenza stopped to covet a polished ripe cashew fruit – within such easy reach, just over the fence – but reminded herself she was on duty. Omar lived high up on the outskirts of Sacha Yacu, surrounded by his grown-up sons and daughters and their families. Far to the south, beyond a belt of dark green forest, the small river that flowed past the village was swept into the Amazon's broad, shimmering torrent. This side was Colombia, the other side was Peru, though where the frontier actually divided the river was a mystery.

The nearer she came to the top of the ridge, the slower Carmenza climbed: not just because it was hard, sweaty work, but because she didn't particularly want to arrive. Manuel might be there with his maddening teasing – or Ramiro, odiously clever and superior, as well as taller and older. The brothers were so different in character, but almost identical to look at, with their broad brown faces and knowing black eyes. Carmenza couldn't decide which of Omar's youngest sons she liked least, and normally went out of her way to avoid them.

Unfortunately, it wasn't easy to avoid Manuel – she sat next to him in the front row at school, put there by a teacher who found it was the only way to get any attention from the shirkers. Carmenza's snub-nose and dark eyebrows crinkled uncharacteristically into a frown as she remembered the studying she had promised to do in between message runs.

"Here comes the spider, the spider, the spindly legged spider!" taunted a voice hidden in a tree.

"Spiders are hairy – I'm not!" shouted Carmenza, infuriated.

"Then it must be a frog, a frog, a pop-eyed frog," chanted the voice. "A clammy-skinned, pot-bellied frog!"

Carmenza, who was used to Manuel's baiting, tried to shut it out, unaware that she had already given him the satisfaction of pulling in her stomach.

"Is your father in? I have a message for him."

"What is it? I'll tell him," said Manuel, aiming a seed pod at the yellow slide that kept Carmenza's floppy brown hair out of her eyes.

"No, *I* have to." For once she was glad the operator insisted that every message must be delivered directly to the person concerned. There had been one or two ghastly mix-ups when go-betweens had mangled the instructions: Carmenza was blamed the day the mayor waited in vain for a delegation of government officials to arrive in Sacha Yacu, instead of going eighty kilometres down the River Amazon to meet them in Leticia. Somehow, his wife had turned the message around when she'd relayed it.

"Then you can swim out to the lake to find him. Father's fishing," said Manuel triumphantly. "And I bet he catches more than your father does!"

Carmenza fled down the hill, unwilling to defend her step-father, or even to argue that he wasn't her real father. Of course he'd never be as good a fisherman as Omar – he'd only come to the Amazon from his mountain farm three years ago. And Omar was pure Indian, so small and bow-legged that he looked as if he'd spent his life in a canoe.

The palm trees' shadows stretched across the football pitch on the water-front, and Carmenza could see evening bathers splashing in the river. A swim was tempting – so much so that all thoughts of homework evaporated instantly. She jumped over a small canoe lying on the bank and ran along until she was opposite a rotting wooden raft which had already lost some of its planks. In the mornings, women kneeled on the edge washing clothes. Now her friend Ana and two others were climbing on to it, laughing and pushing each other back into the water.

Carmenza kicked off her sandals and flung herself into the river, skirt, blouse and all. Swimsuits were rarely seen in Sacha Yacu – small kids bathed naked and everyone else kept a few clothes on.

The water was a dense soupy brown;

there might be anything lurking an arm's length away. But to Carmenza it was delicious, and the deeper she pushed her toes the cooler it felt.

"Watch out, a dolphin! It might kidnap you!" called Ana from the raft.

Carmenza swam over and pulled herself out hurriedly. She wasn't worried about the dolphin, but an electric eel living under the raft was another matter. Jumping in, you could throw yourself way out into the river. Getting out was scary, though, particularly those last few moments when legs still dangled in the water.

"Where?" she asked, then saw from Ana's face that it had been a joke.

"I'm not afraid of dolphins, not even the pink ones," said Carmenza firmly. "They don't do any harm, and my uncle told me that his puppy was saved by a grey one when it fell out of the canoe."

"Ha, so you wouldn't mind if they carried you down to the underwater world?" teased Ana. "You know, where dolphins have siestas in anaconda hammocks and wear hats like stingrays? And what about the handsome ones that come out at night, and dance with you and make you fall in love with them?"

Carmenza made a silly face and flicked at a floating twig with her big toe. She was remembering the foreigners who had come to Sacha Yacu the year before to capture three dolphins for a zoo. The men had smiled uncomfortably at the dolphin stories, unsure whether to take them seriously. Then they'd caught a little grey one – a Sotalia, they'd called this smaller kind of dolphin – and two large pink and grey Inia. When she saw the animals lying uncomfortably on canvas stretchers in the bottom of a boat, Carmenza had felt sad for their helplessness. The Sotalia had died, she'd heard, before it had even reached Leticia. Sometimes she imagined the Inia dolphins on the other side of the world, homesick for the Amazon.

The girls rolled over on the raft and squinted upstream into the setting sun, bickering about who had scored most points in the last basketball game. Two figures in a small canoe were silhouetted against the gleaming water. It was Omar and Ramiro, returning with their fish. Carmenza jumped in and struck out after them for the river-bank.

"Who's this mermaid?" said Omar, his grainy, seamed face wrinkling into a smile. Carmenza gave him the message – unlike most of Sacha Yacu's inhabitants when they got a message, Omar seemed neither curious nor pleased to receive his.

"I hope it's not another anthropologist wanting me to give away all my secrets," he said, leaving Carmenza wondering if he would bother to turn up at the radio room the next day. Ramiro collected the paddle, the spear, the big yellowy-red gamitana and a knife, and walked away across the grass without a word.

Carmenza danced free of a cloud of mosquitoes and took off for home, telling herself she didn't care whether Ramiro noticed her or not.

"Late, of course; I can see you've been fooling around in the river," scolded Carmenza's mother. "And you've lost that pretty yellow slide – typical!" She didn't look as cross as she sounded. "Come on, your father's here and it's time to eat."

"Carlos is *not* my father," muttered Carmenza, loud enough for Blanca, her sister, to hear.

"Shut up, things are bad enough tonight without you stirring it up," admonished Blanca, admiring her frosted fingernails. She was learning hairdressing through her job in Sacha Yacu's beauty parlour, which had neither running water nor electricity. Most of her time was spent experimenting on her own hair – today it was reddish and frizzy. "What a mess you look," she said to Carmenza.

Neither of the girls remembered much about their real father, a river trader from Brazil who came up to Sacha Yacu so seldom that he was hardly missed when he failed to reappear. Although Carlos was quite hard on Blanca, making her be in by ten o'clock on Saturday dance nights, she didn't seem to resent it, and was always trying to smooth out family rows.

They ate their meals in the large half-open kitchen at the back. Carlos was constantly saying he must board up the back wall and turn it into a proper room, but they all preferred it as it was. Along one side there was a wood cooking stove, and three tubs for collecting rain-water stood under the edge of the tin roof.

Carlos had finished his plate of fish and fried plantains. Instead of going out for his usual game of pool he sat jiggling Orlando, the baby, on his lap. Heavy-set, with a thatch of thick, curly black hair, Carlos was unfailingly gentle to Orlando and extraordinarily bad-tempered with everyone else.

"Did you get paid?" he asked Carmenza.

"Tomorrow . . . Mami says I can get a new pair of shoes – look!" She thrust forward her sandalled foot, displaying the torn straps.

"Those can be mended, they'll do for a bit," said Carlos roughly.

Blanca kicked Carmenza under the table and smiled placatingly at Carlos. "Have they stopped work on the water project again?" she asked. Sacha Yacu's drinking-water plant had been under construction for as long as anyone could remember, and Carlos had an intermittent job with the builders.

"Why do you think I've been hanging around at home? D'you imagine I like fishing when there's nothing to catch?"

Carmenza couldn't resist a dig. "Omar

came in with a beautiful gamitana. He doesn't even have a net."

"That old witch doctor!" thundered Carlos so violently that Orlando began to whimper. "He probably casts spells to catch fish . . . and women too, look at all the children he's got. I've a good mind to get myself a dolphin tooth . . . All these tricky Indians have them as charms."

"You can't do that!" said Carmenza, horrified, and Blanca cut in quickly:

"It's terribly dangerous, only the Indians know the right way to use them."

"You're just as superstitious as they are – I suppose you get it from Zoila's family." He glared at their mother. "The next thing, you'll be telling me that dolphins can turn into people. I don't believe any of that rubbish, and if we're going to eat while I'm out of work, we need fish, and if it takes a charm to catch them, I'll kill a dolphin for its tooth!"

The boat

The net stretched from a thick vine by the bank to a half-submerged post further up the inlet. Several fish were struggling to free themselves from the nylon mesh. Others, caught soon after Carlos set the net the evening before, had been devoured by piranhas. Now the red-bellied piranhas were back for a second easy meal. They tore at the fish, and their razor-sharp teeth slashed holes in the net.

Two Inia dolphins – one entirely pink, apart from his brown streak, the other dark grey all along her back, and pale underneath – sensed the piranhas feeding. With a few powerful strokes of their tail-flukes, the dolphins put on a spurt and snapped up the piranhas.

As dawn broke they swam lazily down

a twisting, forest-lined channel to the lower lake, touching flippers occasionally, clicking constantly to check for obstacles. Four neat Sotalia dolphins overtook them, performing showy leaps through the early morning mist that drifted across the water's surface.

The Inia kept close to the flooded bushes along the lakeside, rising to breathe every forty seconds or so. Unhurried, they moved into the river and passed Sacha Yacu as Ramiro and Manuel cleaned their teeth in the shallows after a morning wash. Neither of Omar's youngest sons saw the dolphins.

Minutes later the Inia reached the mouth of the river, where clouds of dark, turbid water billowed into the caramel Amazon, causing a mass of ripples and whirlpools. They joined the Sotalia feasting on fish at the meeting of the waters. Then they bobbed at the surface, using their tail-flukes just enough to stay in the same place while the river flowed past. The male rode down on the current for a little way, rolling luxuriously and waving a flipper in the air. The female began feeding again: the baby inside her had been growing for more than ten months and would soon be born.

The steady whine of a powerful outboard motor was picked up by the dolphins long before a human ear would have registered it. By the time the boat approached the narrow river-mouth, the noise – higher pitched underwater – was enveloping the dolphins. The pink male, attracted by the water swirling out from the propeller, swam close behind it, a game he had often enjoyed before.

But suddenly the boatman saw patches of mist upriver and cut the motor to half-speed. Although the pink dolphin turned sharply aside, he was not quick enough. The propeller blade glanced his jaw in an explosion of pain.

Plans

The mist had evaporated by the time
Carlos set out for the lake to check
his net, and an early morning smell of
rotting vegetation hung along the river-
bank among the huge buttressed trees.
Two canoes passed him: Indians heading
for the forest vegetable gardens where
they grew bananas, plantains, maize and
manioc roots. Even after three years in
the Amazon Carlos never felt entirely
comfortable on the water, and often
longed for the crisp, mosquito-free Andes
mountains. But his family's plot of land
had become too small to feed them all;
two of his brothers had gone to look for
work in the capital, and he had heard of
a cousin who was supposed to be making
a fortune in Leticia.

The fortune turned out to be a shack-like bar on the waterfront, a meeting-place for Colombian, Brazilian and Peruvian traders, just as Leticia itself was the meeting-point for the three countries. Even the frontier language had become a curious blend of Spanish and Portuguese, with a few Indian words thrown in.

His cousin was clearly relieved when Carlos finally decided to go up the Amazon to Sacha Yacu with the idea of farming. Carlos winced at the memory of his brief farming efforts – carving a patch out of the forest couldn't have been less like planting potatoes on open highland hillsides. A week of breaking his back in the midst of twisting creepers and densely growing tree-trunks earned Carlos only a small gap in the green canopy overhead. It also gave him an agonising crop of bee-stings, ant-bites and nasty infected blisters. By comparison, the job on the water project was just ordinary hard work.

As soon as Carlos untied his net, the slackness told him there wasn't much of a catch. He pulled the plastic floats into his boat, growing angrier with every armful. Not only was the net empty, but the mesh had been shredded in at least a dozen places.

Carlos swore loudly at the opaque river-surface and fumed his way home through the humid morning. That it was illegal to fish with large nets in the lake did not bother him for a moment. Twice, dolphins came up to breathe near him, so low in the water that they looked like caimans sliding along. His anger gradually crystal-lised into a conviction that the dolphins had stolen his fish and damaged his net, and were now making fun of him.

Carlos threw down the net on the kitchen floor.

"You're so good with a sewing machine, see if you can repair that," he said to Zoila, who knew better than to argue that nets couldn't be mended on a machine. "And let's hope that daughter of yours brings her radio money home today. It's time they paid Blanca at that ridiculous beauty parlour too."

Although she didn't like asking for help, and had supported herself and the girls for years through dressmaking, Zoila took the net straight around to her brother, Juan.

He was unsympathetic. "Serves you right for taking in a stray outsider who can't even hit a pool ball straight. And what a prize idiot, leaving his net out all night for the piranhas." Juan grinned meanly. "Tell you what, I'll lend him a harpoon while I'm fixing this and we'll see whether he's man enough to bring in a pirarucú."

Zoila pulled at her ear doubtfully – only an experienced fisherman could harpoon the giant pirarucú when the lakes were flooded. Once the water-level dropped

26

it became much easier, because the fish were concentrated in a smaller area. But, she thought, a pirarucú – well salted to preserve it – would feed the family for two weeks.

So Zoila accepted the long, heavy harpoon with its cruelly spiked iron head, and stood it behind the front door when she got home. The midday heat had become so intense that she wasn't surprised to find Orlando sprawled on top of Carlos in the hammock, both sleeping noisily.

Carmenza arrived and collapsed limply on a bench, fanning herself with an exercise book.

"We've been sent home early – the teachers say it's too hot to bear us. Is there something to drink?"

"Get me that cupuassú and I'll make some juice," said her mother, ladling water out of a tub. "If it doesn't rain soon we'll have to start boiling the river-water."

Carmenza used a long stick to prod the cupuassú off its branch, and caught the big brown fruit as it fell. She stared up hopefully into the tall pomarosa tree at the end of the yard. A glittering green humming-bird darted between the last few shocking-pink flowers – it was too early for the fruit. She watered Zoila's small herb garden, planted in the remnants of a canoe which perched out of reach of the chickens on two forked supports. The coriander and onions were for flavouring, the peppermint to soothe the stomach, and verbena tea helped Blanca's head-aches. Zoila, who had learned herb lore from her Indian mother, often used home remedies instead of the expensive pills prescribed at the health centre.

Carlos's snoring from the hammock was becoming stronger than ever, and Car-menza couldn't resist tickling Orlando's toes. She regretted it, for with loud coughing and snuffling, the baby kicked himself awake, and roused a grumpy Carlos too.

"There's something for you over there." Zoila nodded towards the front door. "From my brother Juan, for catching pirarucú."

Carlos hefted the harpoon in his right hand, and examined the strong line attached to the head. Not just for pirarucú, he thought vengefully. But Blanca's arrival diverted his attention. Expecting him to be out, she had left her skirt hitched up to mid-thigh and was wearing luscious red lipstick, strictly against Carlos's orders. Carmenza, on her way out to the radio, was pleased to see the fury break on her sister's head for a change.

The heat was still blasting down; Sacha Yacu's inhabitants moved about as little as possible, and the radio operator drooped over her equipment. She sent Carmenza off to collect the money for unpaid calls, warning that

29

her fortnightly wages depended on the result. Carmenza was used to this, and blackmailed people without shame, telling them they wouldn't get messages unless they paid up.

She pocketed some money from Don Miguel, who owned the biggest shop in Sacha Yacu – a wonderful place bursting with food bins, saucepans, machetes, rope, candles, pencils, Brazilian champagne and sweets. Then, remembering the essay question she'd been given for homework, she asked the people waiting to use the radio why the next day – September the first – was an important date. One woman said it was her daughter's birthday, another thought some president of Colombia had been assassinated, and a soldier from the base up the river told Carmenza she was so ignorant she didn't deserve to know.

At three o'clock Omar's call came through, but the old man hadn't arrived.

"Go and get *somebody* from that family," said the operator. "They're going to try again in an hour."

Carmenza climbed the hill, watching the trees at the top and the hibiscus bushes for an ambush by Manuel. There didn't seem to be anyone at home and she was about to give up when Manuel appeared with two baby parrots cupped in his hands. He was so absorbed in the birds that he forgot to be obnoxious.

"I had to climb incredibly high to get to the nest," he boasted. "I'm giving them mashed bananas." Carmenza stroked the small frightened creatures. They were almost entirely green, with a faint trace of red over the hooked beaks and blue around the eyes.

"Isn't anyone else home?" she asked. "Somebody wants your father on the radio."

"They're all out by the lake, making a new garden. I'll come." Manuel was

31

delighted to have the chance to talk on the radio, and shoved his parrots quickly away into a basket.

The voice came through strongly. Carmenza – eavesdropping as usual – heard the caller say he needed a guide who knew the forest, and room and board for two people in Sacha Yacu. Manuel, forgetting that only one person could speak at a time, kept trying to interrupt. The conversation became more and more confused – evidently the man in Leticia thought he was talking to Omar; he said everything seemed fine, he'd be there on Friday, and they would meet then.

Manuel shrugged rudely when Carmenza asked him what he intended to do. "It's none of your business," he said, and of course it wasn't. Manuel was already planning: Omar was too old for forest trekking and would suggest Ramiro as a guide. Supposing Manuel said nothing about the call, he could pretend Omar had sent him to meet the visitors . . . and – Wow! – there would be fun and money and presents. They might even give him a shot-gun if he arranged some good hunting!

Carmenza was planning too. She dashed home as soon as the radio shut down, ignoring an invitation from Ana to play basketball. Outsiders were rare enough in Sacha Yacu to be interesting – and few enough for there to be no hotel. Breathlessly, Carmenza explained her idea to her mother.

"They can stay in Aunt Sonia's house, and they'll be close by, so you can cook for them. They're bound to be rich, and they'll have to pay you for everything!"

Zoila shifted Orlando from one breast to the other and he went on sucking greedily.

"I wonder . . . Sonia and the kids won't

be back from Leticia until school finishes . . . We could put the two beds in the front room, that should be good enough for them. Yes!" She smiled at Carmenza, who was distracting Orlando with clownish faces, and switched to her stern look. "I met your teacher today. She's fed up with you, says you never do any homework . . . Well?"

Carmenza knew her mother wouldn't stop her working because they needed the money. "I never have any time . . . oh, my homework! Do you know why September the first is so special? What happened?"

"Of course I do . . . Haven't I told you about my teacher, the one who started the first school ever in the Colombian Amazon?"

"No . . . yes," said Carmenza, puzzled. "What's she got to do with it?"

"She was over the river in Caballococha when the Peruvians were training to attack Leticia. I think she was taking a holiday –

Caballococha was the biggest town in the region in those days – but anyway, the Peruvians thought she must be a spy. They said she had to leave in three days or they'd put her on an island in the middle of the Amazon, with nothing but wild animals for company.

"So she went back to Leticia and told the governor what she'd seen – but he said she should keep quiet and forget it. He didn't believe the Peruvians would attack, and he didn't want to frighten people who'd come from other parts of Colombia to settle down. They'd planted crops, and some were in the rubber business . . .

"On September the first – it was in 1932 – the Peruvians swooped across and there weren't even any soldiers in Leticia: they'd all been re-posted to another part of the frontier. The governor was in his pyjamas! Well, who knows if that was really true. Anyway, the Peruvians took down the

Colombian flag, and hoisted their own red and white one, and sent most of the Colombians over the border into Brazil. In the end, Peru had to give Leticia back, of course. My teacher worked in all sorts of out-of-the-way places, up and down the rivers, but in the end she came back and organised a school for the Indian kids in Arara, where we lived.

"There – have I done your homework?" asked Zoila, dropping her story-telling voice and looking pleased with herself.

Carmenza nodded gratefully. "I'll write all that in class tomorrow . . . Is she still alive?"

"I don't know, she'd be very old. All right, off you go and bathe now. But take your money out of your pocket first – and I'm afraid the shoes will have to wait, we're a bit short with Carlos out of work."

Carmenza stopped at the water's edge to examine a canoe full of black-patterned catfish which were being bought up by un-lucky fishermen. She took a running jump into the water and floated out, letting the current carry her down to one of the boat-houses anchored near the bank. There was petrol on the water, forming oily rings around some drifting orange petals, so she swam farther across. A sudden rasping breath gave her a moment's panic, until she realised it was just a noisy dol-phin. But it had reminded her of the elec-tric eel and other creatures she couldn't see ... Then she felt a large body bump against her, and almost screamed. The dolphin breathed hoarsely once again. This time, as she splashed for the bank, she saw a pink head with a horribly maimed mouth.

The river crossing

"Well, today's September the first, and I hope you've all got something interesting to say about it," said the nun in charge of the two classes. They were all jammed together in the same room, which made it difficult to keep control when two sets of lessons were going on, but the plump, spectacled nun was fiercer than she looked. Her spotless white habit swished down the rows as she handed out paper.

Carmenza glanced at Manuel wriggling restlessly in his seat, and for once set to work with gusto, re-telling her mother's version of the attack on Leticia.

The other side of the room, among the older group, Ramiro had also begun writing. He became so wrapped up in his story that he forgot to mention September 1st.

"My father's name is Omar. He is more than seventy years old, and he was mixed up in the war with Peru. But he wasn't a soldier, because he was younger then than I am now.

"His mother was a Ticuna Indian, and his father was a Witoto Indian, and they lived on the Colombian side of the Putumayo river. They had to collect rubber from the trees in the forest, and take it to the Peruvians. If they didn't bring enough rubber, the white men beat them and threw them into the river and the caimans ate them. My father's uncle died like that.

"Then the war started and the Peruvians went back to Peru. They forced all the Indian families to go with them, otherwise they said they would kill them. My father went with his parents and brothers and sisters. None of them knew which was

Peru and which was Colombia, or why there was a war. They had to collect rubber, the same as before, and they lived in camps like prisons, going from one to another. In one of the camps everyone caught a terrible fever, and all my father's family died of it. My father still had to collect rubber in the forest.

"One day he escaped from the guards. He was a long way from the Putumayo river, but he met some Witoto Indians who had escaped too, and they travelled through the forest together. My father already knew how to hunt monkeys and deer and tapir.

"When they arrived at the Putumayo river, the Witoto decided to make a canoe so they could cross over and paddle along the river to their village. My father thought it would take a long time to find the right tree and cut it down and make the canoe. He was sure the Peruvians would find them. He told the

Witoto that he would cross the river on his own, and they thought he was crazy.

"He stood on the river-bank and waited until the middle of the day when the sun was exactly over his head. That is the time when the caimans are dozy. He whistled in a special way, and some dolphins came close to the river-bank.

"My father got into the water, and the current was too strong, it carried him away. But the dolphins swam on either side of him. They saved him from the caimans and the whirlpools and the piranhas, and he crossed over and went on through the forest to his village. There was nothing there any more, and he wandered for a long time before he came to the Amazon.

"He can still call the dolphins."

A giant fish

It was Friday, and it hadn't rained for ten days. The water was dropping, exposing naked roots, muddy banks and enormous trees which had fallen into the river during the floods. Distant thunder gave hope of rain-showers, but it just got hotter.

Omar's family was clearing a patch of forest near the big lake for a new garden. The biggest trees had already been cut down, carrying with them dozens of smaller ones as they crashed to the earth. The vegetation would be burned once it had dried out, then planting would begin.

Although some manioc and fruit trees were still growing in the old garden, the soil was exhausted after three harvests, and the maize plants remained stunted, with yellowish leaves. It had been difficult finding a suitable spot to clear – not too far from Sacha Yacu, but in long-standing forest – because most of the best places had already been farmed at one time or another, and the forest took a long time to recover.

Omar's three older sons and their wives had come to help, as well as two of his daughters. In all, fifteen people were working on different tasks. The women cut palm fronds to roof the shelter being put up by the men. Ramiro, who had paddled out in his canoe after school, chopped steps into a log. When the planks were laid, the floor of the shelter would be more than a metre above ground, and the log would lean against it, providing a staircase.

Everyone stopped work for a while and squatted in the shade. They talked about the tree-trunks that lay littered all over the garden, and what they might be used for;

about the plants and animals they had noticed near the garden; and about how far they had to travel in order to hunt for their families when the fish weren't biting. The women passed around gourds of thick, satisfying manioc beer. Omar was always at the centre of the group, and nobody interrupted when he spoke, but much of the time he stayed silent and let his children laugh and argue among themselves. He was pleased that the shelter was nearly finished – he would live in it, partly to take care of the crops they planted, and partly because he wanted to be on his own, away from Sacha Yacu. His wife would paddle out often to work in the garden – she was younger than he and enjoyed being among her family.

Omar had told Ramiro he would be welcome at any time – Ramiro understood that his father was ordering him to come, and felt proud. He was the only member of the family who could read and write the Ticuna language, as well as Spanish. But he kept quiet about things like that; his classmates thought it ridiculous to write in Ticuna, and were ashamed to speak it in front of anyone who wasn't Indian. Ramiro also knew how to make a fishing spear, where to find plants for curing fevers, and which wood to use for a strong paddle. Unlike Manuel, he preferred Omar's stories to the violent films shown in Sacha Yacu when the mayor sent for video-tapes from Leticia. His younger brother was so uncooperative, thought Ramiro, he hadn't even come to help clear the garden which would grow his food.

Ramiro would have been even more critical if he could have seen Manuel at that moment. He was waiting impatiently on the highest part of the bank at Sacha Yacu, watching the distant rivermouth for a boat. He had slicked down his black hair, and wore a shirt, which was most unusual and would have raised questions from his mother. He had also borrowed his brother's cap: the faded flags and lettering announced it was a present to celebrate friendship between the three Amazon frontier nations.

Carmenza had noticed him because she too was keeping an eye on the river, popping out of the radio room every few minutes. Two new red slides held her hair back, and her embroidered blouse was neatly belted into her skirt.

When the boat finally appeared, it was exactly what they'd both expected: a fast fibreglass launch with an impressive bow-wave rearing up either side of the prow.

Manuel stood knee-deep in the water, ready to help pull in the boat and act as guide. Carmenza ran up as two young men in dark glasses and rubber boots got out.

"My mother's waiting to show you where you're staying," volunteered Carmenza.

"I'll carry your luggage," said Manuel,

then regretted the offer when he realised how much there was.

"Wait a minute, how do you know who we are anyway?" asked the taller, heavier man.

"I'm Omar's son . . . "

"I work at the radio . . . " they answered together.

"Ah . . . well, I'm Pablo," said the thin one with the moustache, "and this is Roberto. I guess we might as well see the room first of all. Will you look after our stuff?"

Manuel nodded, and Carmenza led the way through the small crowd of people who had gathered to inspect the strangers and admire the boat.

They said Zoila's arrangements would suit them fine, provided they could use the backyard. Several onlookers started unloading the baggage in the hope of latching on to this enterprise, whatever it might be – Pablo, in his nattily cut khaki trousers and jungle shirt, looked very prosperous. Manuel became more and more anxious: the adults seemed to be taking over before he'd made his bargain with the visitors. When Pablo came back to organise the storage of five large petrol drums in the boathouse, Manuel announced that he was ready to take them into the forest as soon as they wanted.

"Aren't you a bit young for a guide?" teased Pablo. "What would happen if a puma attacked us?"

"You'd shoot it," said Manuel confidently. He'd seen the shot-gun case amongst the sacks, bags, coolers and boxes.

"We hoped Omar would work with us. A friend of ours who came to Sacha Yacu a few years ago told us he was good with a blow-gun, and a first-class tracker."

"He's old now. Nobody here uses blow-guns any more," said Manuel. "I know where to find animals, that's what you want, isn't it?"

"Well . . . partly, yes, but there's no need to shout it around." Pablo considered Manuel, and took off his dark glasses to reveal a pair of pale hazel eyes. "Supposing we do try you out . . . what's your rate?"

Manuel was ready for that. "A pair of sneakers from Don Miguel's shop. And when you go, you can leave me some of your things." He decided not to mention the gun yet.

"We'll expect you at five in the morning then." Pablo chained the boat to a tree-trunk, and wandered off to nose around Sacha Yacu. When he returned to Sonia's house, Blanca was hanging up rain-capes, trying to disguise her curiosity by being useful. Large gilt rings flashed in her ears. After asking a string of questions and getting rather short answers, she told the visitors that food would be ready at seven, apologising in advance for Sacha Yacu's limited cooking.

"It's all right, I like fish and plantains," said Pablo with a wink, causing Blanca's heart to bounce up into her throat. Speechless at last, she swayed down the path.

Zoila flapped around the kitchen, chopping onions, sending Carmenza to the baker's, and trying to control Orlando, who was experimenting exuberantly with his first wobbly steps.

"Carmenza, get him out of here right away," she said, grabbing Orlando just before he dived into the cooking fire.

"Shall I take him for a bathe?"

"I don't care what you do, just go! And tell Blanca to come and help me if she's willing to leave her mirror for a moment and dirty her hands." Zoila yelped as she turned a charred plantain.

By the time Carmenza reached the river, she was glad to put chubby Orlando down. She sat him in a small untended canoe and swam towards the raft where Ana and the others were playing, pushing the canoe ahead of her. The bank reached closer to the raft every day, and if the water continued to drop, they'd soon be walking out to it.

Carmenza's friends lifted Orlando out, delighted to play with him. He had no fear of the water, and when Ana held him by the wrists and ducked him over the edge of the raft, he came up spluttering and giggling.

"Shall we send you to the dolphin world?" laughed Ana, hugging him.

The last of the sunlight glowed on families arriving from their gardens in heavily laden canoes, so low in the water that the slightest tilt could overturn them. A dog followed one canoe, swimming with its ears pointing high above the surface. It was cool at last, with a breeze from the south – so much so that Carmenza felt a sudden chilliness surge through her.

Orlando was covered with goose-pimples and no longer enjoying himself, so she pushed him back to the bank and lugged him home.

The table – its stains hidden by their best blue cloth – was ready for the visitors. Carmenza noticed that Zoila had cooked far more than two people could eat and looked forward to the leftovers. She was chasing cockroaches around the kitchen, under Zoila's instructions to kill as many as possible, when Carlos came raging into the house.

He flung down a long, heavy pole. They all recognised it as the harpoon shaft.

"So much for your brother's workmanship," he accused Zoila. "Somewhere in that lake there's a fiendish pirarucú with a spike in it."

Despite the loss of the harpoon head, Zoila was impressed that Carlos had managed to strike a pirarucú at all. "What happened?" she asked.

With his first anger exploded, Carlos calmed down. He sat on the bench, leaning forward, elbows on thighs and chin cupped in his hands. Zoila gave him a glass of fruit juice.

"It's been a long day. I paddled out to the lake mid-morning. There were quite a few fishermen around the end of the channel. To get well away from them I went all along the right-hand side. You know how far that is." They nodded. "It was terribly hot, no breeze, the sun pounding down. I paddled into the shade, under the trees, and there were lots of small fish catching insects to eat. But I wanted a pirarucú.

"Twice I saw pirarucús on the surface, slapping their great tails and splashing all over the place, but I was too far away. Then, later, the wind began to blow from the end of the lake. I was half in, half out of the shadow of the trees, moving along very slowly, so quietly, the paddle in my left hand, the harpoon in my right.

"The wind was ruffling the surface, so it was difficult to see anything coming up. I paddled out into the sunlight again, thinking it might be better. Just at that moment, right in line with the sun, a small wave splashed over a pirarucú. It was about two canoe-lengths away – a good chance, even though I was nearly blinded. I threw with all my strength, aiming forwards and downwards.

"The fish swam off crazily, taking the line with it. Really, it must have been huge. I could see the float going all over the place on the surface. I picked the shaft out of the water, and the pirarucú pulled me one way, then the other. It swam under the canoe – I thought I'd tip over any moment. Then – snap – and suddenly I was sitting still, holding a useless harpoon, and not a float in sight."

"Sounds as if it was a good fight. Maybe we could use help from someone like you," said Pablo, who had been standing unnoticed in the dark doorway for several minutes.

The spike

The pink dolphin felt nothing but pain.

For days he had been unable to fish because of his mutilated jaw. It had begun to heal, but he was weak and the blow from the outboard motor had affected the sound beam he used to sense objects and find his way. He relied almost entirely on echo-location in the dark lake water so he was both disoriented and vulnerable.

In this confused state, he surfaced briefly to breathe near a canoe. As he sank, an agonising burning seared through his side and held him. He dived back and forth under the canoe, frantic to tear himself away. With every move he made, the savage pain seemed to cut deeper, until at last the tugging stopped and he was swimming free. Trailing from his right flipper was a cord attached to the double-headed iron spike embedded in his flesh. Carlos had plunged the harpoon into a particularly sensitive area, just where the flipper joined the dolphin's flank.

A muddy slope finally stopped his erratic flight. His mate was the first to reach him, and she scanned his body agitatedly, seeking the damage. She nosed at the cord and found the base of the harpoon head emerging from a ragged, bleeding tear.

Two more Inia circled close by. The wounded dolphin hung still underwater, making no attempt to go up for air. He was in shock, and would die unless he rose to breathe. His mate swam underneath, and nudged the body gently upwards. Another Inia lifted the tail in the same way, and the pink dolphin gradually floated to the surface. They kept him there, shielded by a curtain of dangling vines and branches, near the bank. At last he opened his blow-hole and breathed out, then in.

With consciousness, pain returned. The Inias supported him and drove away piranhas and other fishes drawn by the smell of blood in the water. Further out in the lake three more dolphins patrolled protectively all through the night.

By dawn the pink dolphin was able to move on his own. But the new injury to his flipper had disabled him so badly that he could neither steer nor swim properly. How was he to fish, and build up the strength he had already lost as a result of starving for days?

Then an even worse thing happened. The harpoon cord, which was several metres long, looped itself around the roots and trunks in the shallow water where the dolphin lay. He tried to swim clear, but the cord tightened and the iron head dug deeper into him. He was trapped.

Omacha

Orlando cried and cried and cried, getting on everyone's nerves. He was red and uncomfortable and wouldn't eat. They took turns trying to soothe or distract him but it was hopeless. There didn't seem to be anything specific wrong, so Zoila left him swinging in the hammock while she cleaned the kitchen.

She was pleased because Pablo and Roberto had praised her cooking, and they'd asked Carlos to join them for the day. She still didn't understand exactly what they were doing in Sacha Yacu, though she had her suspicions... Blanca had flirted dreadfully the evening before and Zoila smiled to herself when she remembered Carmenza's disgusted expression.

"Who's that yelling his head off?" The voice startled Zoila, who turned to find Roberto in the kitchen.

"Oh . . . Orlando's very crotchety – but I thought you'd all gone off into the forest today?"

"Pablo went with Carlos and Manuel. I decided to try and get hold of Omar. I forgot to ask Manuel where I'd find him – any ideas?"

"Carmenza might know – she's free, there's no radio service at the weekend. Try the waterfront."

Roberto found Carmenza with Ana, hacking open some coconuts and drinking the contents thirstily. She took him up to Omar's house, her tatty sandals making much quicker progress than his elegant leather boots.

Ramiro answered the door, and started to explain about the new garden, but Roberto interrupted:

"Why don't you show me – the boat's ready."

Ramiro had a feeling his father wasn't going to like the invasion – after all he was moving out to the lake to get away from people – but it was difficult to refuse. Carmenza went along for the ride, and annoyed Ramiro by waving self-importantly at anyone who cared to look as they roared upriver into the lower lake.

She enjoyed every moment, particularly winding through the channel to the big lake. The water had fallen far enough to reveal holes made by black catfish in the mud-bank, and Roberto had to slow down to avoid the fallen trees with pretty bluey-grey tanagers perching on them. Four Sotalia dolphins jumped ahead of the boat, then disappeared and came up behind them. A great tree with dozens of birds' nests hanging down from its branches thrust high above the rest of the canopy, and two hawks hovered hopefully nearby, their brown and white speckled bellies barely visible against the brilliant sky.

The garden was about half-way along the right side of the lake, behind a belt of forest. They climbed over logs and around piles of drying vegetation to the shelter. It was already half-roofed and Omar was cutting long straight saplings into poles to support the palm fronds for the other half.

He greeted Roberto politely and spoke to Ramiro in Ticuna, but carried on working. Each stroke of the machete was so precise, each notch so neat that Ramiro was astonished to think his father's eyesight could be failing. They all stood around awkwardly until Omar put down his machete.

"I haven't had time to go fishing this morning – take my canoe, Ramiro, and see what you and the girl can find." He got up slowly but steadily and stretched his bent limbs. Beside Roberto, he was tiny, and Carmenza found she was looking almost directly into his brown milky eyes. He smiled teasingly at her. "You're always on the move – I wonder, can you sit still long enough to catch a fish?"

Neither Ramiro nor Carmenza was very keen on the arrangement, but somehow one didn't argue with Omar, and he obviously wanted them out of the way while he talked with Roberto. Ramiro picked up the paddle, machete and spear and went straight to the canoe. Carmenza sat in the stern with nothing to do except study the foliage, watch the terns or slap at insects. She certainly didn't find it easy to keep still, and irritated Ramiro with her constant fidgeting – though he said nothing. They drifted along under the trees, the noise of the crickets punctuated by the occasional splash as Ramiro threw the spear. Each time he recovered it there was a twitching fish on the end. Inia dolphins came up to breathe nearby, making a sad, sighing sound.

"What's that?" said Carmenza, pointing at a bobbing float. "Somebody's net?"

Ramiro frowned, but paddled through the creepers to investigate. He hauled the float into the canoe; at once it was pulled out again, and they felt the water swirling fiercely under them. Carmenza cried out when the dolphin's pink head appeared.

"He's hurt, look, in the mouth! It's the same one I saw in the river the other day!"

The dolphin had already gone under. They were close enough to make out a large pale shape in the shallow water. Ramiro reached for the float again, taking greater care not to jerk it.

"He must be caught on this – maybe there's a fishing hook on the end." Hand over hand, Ramiro gathered in the slack until he felt resistance on the line. He was about to cut it, but Carmenza stopped him.

"Don't do that – as long as the float's

on we can tell where the dolphin is." She peered down into the water. "If we could make him go right to the bank we'd see what's the matter."

Although the dolphin was far more wary of humans now than he had been before the harpoon struck, he had to come up for air or die. He rose as far away from the canoe as possible, which put him closer to the trees growing along the edge of the lake.

"I've seen him before too," said Ramiro. "I recognise his colour – so pink, with that odd brownish streak." He remembered Omar's relief that he hadn't harmed the dolphin that day, and it strengthened his determination to try to help. At least Carmenza was behaving sensibly, he thought, girls were often afraid of dolphins, especially pink Inia.

"Well, whatever's on that cord, it's not in his head or his back. It must be stuck

in the tail or one of the flippers," said
Carmenza. "Shall we try and catch him
the next time he comes up?"

Ramiro was doubtful. "He's big, and
dolphins are very strong . . . "

"Well, I don't care. If you won't try, I
will." She dropped the unbarbed end of
the spear into the water to test the depth.
It would be roughly up to her chin, though
she could feel all kinds of obstacles on
the bottom. It would be most unpleasant
standing in that lot, and the mud would
be soft too.

Ramiro couldn't help admiring her.

"First, let's see if he'll go even nearer
the bank, in between those trees. If he
does we can probably stop him coming
out again."

He paddled farther in. After a quick
breath, the pink shape slipped ahead,
followed by the float. As the line tautened,
Ramiro realised it was longer than he had
imagined, allowing the dolphin quite a bit

of movement. Now the outline of the body was plain – they could even trace the contours of the tail and flippers.

The canoe drifted up to the flooded trees, and Ramiro manoeuvred it across the gap between them. The dolphin had placed himself in an almost perfect natural pen, with the bank ahead, a confusion of branches on either side, and two trees guarding the entrance.

"Look," said Carmenza excitedly, "the line goes into that flipper. The hook must be stuck in there." She pushed the spear down again, and found that the water would only reach her waist. "Come on!"

Before Ramiro could answer, she slithered in, upsetting the canoe and tipping Ramiro out too.

"Quick – the machete's sinking," she warned, but he had already grabbed it.

Ramiro moved his feet carefully, feeling for sharp sticks in the slime. He shuffled forward until he was by the dolphin's tail, then leaned over and cut the cord as close to the dolphin's flipper as he could get. The dolphin stayed quiet.

"Do you think he knows we want to help?" wondered Carmenza. There was a tiny movement of the tail, and the dolphin's head came up. Although the blow-hole opened and closed as quickly as ever, the head stayed above the surface and turned slightly. Both Ramiro and Carmenza felt the dolphin's small eye fix on them, almost as if to reassure. They saw the gash in the jaw, and his teeth where the mouth was split open.

"I think he probably does," said Ramiro. "I'm going to feel down the side here."

He touched the dolphin's back – there was no reaction, so he gradually moved his hand down towards the flipper. Carmenza, on the other side, also began to stroke the dolphin's back, hoping to soothe him.

The dolphin shuddered suddenly and shook his head.

"What was that?" asked Carmenza.

"I'm feeling the bit where his flipper goes into the body – it's all torn," said Ramiro. "Wait a minute – I've got the end of the cord, there's a big bit of metal sticking into him." He probed a little farther, but this was just too much for the dolphin. He thrashed his tail wildly, and both Ramiro and Carmenza were thrown off their feet. For the first time, they realised how powerful the great body was. Yet the dolphin hadn't tried to escape.

"It must be a harpoon," said Ramiro, "and it's really deep. I don't know how we could get it out."

Carmenza froze, her eyes staring with horror. She pictured Carlos with the headless shaft, and heard him describing his fight with the pirarucú. Ramiro watched her, understanding she was terribly upset and believing it was because of the dolphin's wound.

"Aieee!" She leaped up in the water, hopping and screeching. "Something's biting me, help!" Absorbed by the dolphin, they had forgotten about all the other animals crawling, swimming, eating and sliding around the edge of the lake.

"Get out – on that branch," ordered Ramiro, wrestling to turn the canoe upright. He started sloshing water out with the paddle, then pulled the canoe under the branches so Carmenza could drop into it.

"Ugh!" She showed him her bleeding ankle. A minute chunk of flesh had been bitten out at the back.

"It must have been a fish, maybe a piranha – better than a snake, anyway." Ramiro realised he didn't sound very concerned, and added: "Does it hurt?"

"No – it gave me a fright though, and I

expect I scared the dolphin. Do you think the piranhas might attack him?"

It hadn't occurred to Ramiro, but of course they might. The dolphin looked so helpless now – apart from lifting his head every minute or so to breathe, he wasn't moving.

"I think we should talk with my father, he knows about dolphins. We'll have to get the harpoon spike out or he won't be able to swim and he'll die."

If Carmenza hadn't been so obsessed by the thought of the headless harpoon shaft, she would have been surprised by Ramiro's unusually forthcoming comments. As it was, she felt vaguely aware that something had changed.

"We lost the fish I had caught," Ramiro went on. "I'll see if I can spear a few more on the way back."

"What about the dolphin? Perhaps he can eat, his mouth is already improving – we'll have to catch some for him too!"

Carmenza cheered up immediately at the idea of doing something useful.

Ramiro began to paddle back the way they had come, but all the fish seemed to have gone into hiding.

"It's not a good time, the middle of the day," he explained.

"I know *that*," snapped Carmenza. "I was born here too, and my mother's half Indian." She saw the friendliness drain out of his face, and looked for something nicer to say. "What shall we call him? Or maybe it's a her?"

"No." Ramiro was sure the dolphin was male, chiefly because of his size. "He's called Omacha." He glanced round at Carmenza. "That means dolphin in the Ticuna language."

"I like it," she confirmed.

They headed for Omar's garden, going faster now that Ramiro had given up fishing, their clothes drying rapidly in the burning sun.

Roberto was waiting impatiently on the bank. Clearly his meeting with Omar had not gone well. He jumped into his boat and signalled Carmenza to follow. She hesitated, looking from Roberto to Ramiro, undecided whether to go.

"I'll be staying here tonight," said Ramiro, "and there's only one canoe."

She nodded. Roberto started the motor, and Carmenza stepped into the boat. Ramiro pushed them out, shouting into her ear: "Don't tell anyone about Omacha!"

The journey

Omar lay on the ground, singing himself into a dream. It was dark, and Ramiro kept their small cooking fire burning, according to Omar's instructions. He had told his father about Omacha and asked for advice, but Omar hadn't given him an answer, nor had he gone to see the dolphin. Ramiro had caught a fish at dusk, throwing a line out from the lake's edge, and he had eaten it all because Omar was fasting. With a full stomach and the monotonous background din of untiring insects, Ramiro began to doze off; startling half-awake when a trumpeter bird called – harshly at first, then dying into a low hum.

Omar had stopped singing: now he felt himself floating down, down in the lake, until he reached a dark hole. He studied the entrance to the tunnel, gathering the strength to set out on this journey. As soon as he entered it, the tunnel opened into a great cave filled with sharp rocks covered in lurid, stinging caterpillars, and soft mossy curtains. It was beautiful but threatening, and he knew he should not linger.

He flew out of the cave, following a small stream-bed which ran on down the tunnel over a series of low waterfalls. Dragonflies zoomed past and short striped snakes coiled by the stream. Omar moved on quickly, and all at once he was floating gently again, out into a broad clear river.

There were four Inia dolphins around him. They led him farther down, towards a city with tall buildings and busy avenues, but no people – only dolphins. A troop of Sotalia raced by under the command of an Inia. Omar and his escort followed them to a huge square with a palace on the far side. They hurried along a corridor of stone pillars to a courtyard where a great pink Inia lay. All the dolphins around him were still and sad. Overhead hung a cloud of stingrays, shadowing the courtyard in gloom.

Omar went up to the sick dolphin. He saw the wounded jaw, which was healing, and the horrible injury at the base of the dolphin's flipper. He saw the iron barbs of the harpoon hooked around inside the flesh, and saw that any attempt to pull out the spike would tear the flipper right away from the flank. But he knew there was a way. He told the dolphin to go on breathing, that he would send helpers.

Omar's Inia guards were angry and closed in on him. They would not allow him to leave unless he healed Omacha. He laughed at them and said Omacha would only live if they let him return.

He told them to take another hostage if they must, but they had to free him to do his work.

Omar stirred and turned towards the fire and slept until dawn.

On the lake

Zoila was frying eggs for breakfast – the hens seemed to be doing their best to provide plenty for the visitors. She was worried about Orlando, who had cried himself into exhaustion and was hardly eating. Carmenza tried to entertain him with some beads, but he didn't respond in his normal enthusiastic way.

"I can't understand it – he was fine on Friday night, you took him down to bathe, didn't you?" recalled Zoila.

"He loved it," said Carmenza, "and I brought him in as soon as it got breezy."

"If today wasn't Sunday I'd take him to the doctor," said Zoila. "But she's bound to be off somewhere with her boyfriend from the army base."

"He seems to have a tummy-ache,

why don't you give him one of your concoctions?" suggested Carmenza. Then: "Good morning." This was directed at Pablo and Roberto, who had arrived for breakfast in their usual smart jungle outfits. They asked after Carlos.

"He's around – he went out to see somebody," Carmenza rattled on. "Manuel says you're buying his baby parrots, and he's going to catch some more ... Are you only collecting birds, or other animals too?"

Roberto raised his eyebrows at Pablo. "Nothing's secret in Sacha Yacu, I see ... except, of course, when you want it passed on ... Why didn't Omar know we were coming?"

"Oh, I gave him your message, but he didn't turn up at the radio, and then Manuel came instead." Carmenza was annoyed that Manuel had made it look as if it was her fault. "Anyway, Omar didn't want to work with you, did he?"

Roberto looked at her sharply. "How do you know?"

"It's obvious, isn't it? He wouldn't put wild birds in cages – nor would Ramiro," she added thoughtfully.

Carlos swaggered into the kitchen looking smug, and sat down opposite Pablo.

"Well, I think I've found just what you want. Somebody who's done a whole lot of hunting recently, and was wondering how to get his stuff down to Leticia to sell. It'd suit him fine to have you buy it here."

"We'll have a look – though birds are a much more profitable business than other animals nowadays. Tourists know it's illegal to buy skins, and the foreign market's not as good as it used to be . . . but if the price is reasonable . . . "

Courteous as ever, they thanked Zoila and left with Carlos. While she washed up the plates in brown river-water, Carmenza wondered whether to tell her mother about Omacha and the harpoon. She still wasn't sure if Carlos had lied about the pirarucú – maybe he really believed he had caught one. On the other hand, he'd talked about getting a dolphin tooth . . . Her thoughts were unexpectedly cut short by Ramiro, beckoning urgently from the doorway. He was dressed in jeans and rubber boots.

"You're to come out with me – my father wants us," he said. Greatly relieved – for she had been afraid Zoila would never let her paddle all the way to the lake on her own – Carmenza put her arms around her mother's waist and begged for the day off.

"And I was counting on you to help with Orlando, and there's the washing, and . . . Oh well, get on then, and let's hope Blanca lends a hand. With these two handsome young visitors in and out, she's amazingly willing to hang around the house." Zoila was pleased to see

Carmenza so friendly with Ramiro, whom she considered polite and responsible.

As soon as they were outside, Ramiro stopped. "We need a net to keep piranhas and other fish out – doesn't your father have one?"

"He's not my father," replied Carmenza automatically. "It's torn, my Uncle Juan is mending it . . . he might have finished by now, let's see."

The net was ready, but Carmenza's uncle didn't want to hand it over until he got his harpoon back. She pleaded, pretending Carlos needed the net in a hurry for a special job with Pablo and Roberto.

"All right – I suppose you're the one who'll be blamed if I don't give it to you."

They ran down to the waterfront, and Ramiro pulled two canoes, his own and Omar's, into the water. "I'm taking mine too so when we've dropped my father's off we can come back this evening – here's a paddle." He used the twine on the end of the net to tie the second canoe to the back thwart, and they both sat in the first one.

An hour later they came out of the channel into the lake. Carmenza thought her arms would drop off, but Ramiro's back was as straight as before. At least it wasn't hot . . . thick clouds massed across the sky, and the wind whipped spray off the dull grey surface.

"Where are all the dolphins?" wondered Carmenza out loud.

"It's just that we can't see them in the choppy water," answered Ramiro. "Those animal smugglers – do you know what they're up to?"

"They're mainly interested in birds. Manuel thinks they're wonderful, he follows Pablo around everywhere."

"Huh . . . my father's upset about that, but Manuel doesn't care."

When they arrived, Omar told them to

rest while he went over the net for flaws. Although she wasn't used to manioc beer, Carmenza drank it down gratefully, and found it restored her energy. Omar squatted beside her, more like a wise gnome than ever.

"You know who threw the harpoon, don't you?" he said. She was too embarrassed to look directly at him. "Now you and Ramiro must make sure the dolphin recovers. I shall help you in my own way. When you have taken out the spike, the dolphin will bleed again, and will need protection. He's weak, and he mustn't swim or his flipper won't heal properly. Place the net carefully." They nodded. "Ramiro, here's the medicine, and a smooth stick which should do the job. Carmenza, see if you can wear my boots." Her feet slopped around uncomfortably but Omar stuffed some leaves in the toes. "That's better than nothing, we can't have you being gobbled up by piranhas. Tuck your trousers in, and I'll get on with my roof-thatching."

Omacha's hiding-place couldn't have been better concealed. The fish were jumping under the trees as they approached it, and Ramiro had speared five before Carmenza reminded him crossly that they weren't on a fishing expedition. Two Inia dolphins surged out towards the canoe when they reached the screen of vines.

"Whew! I thought they'd sink us," said Carmenza. "Perhaps they were looking after Omacha?"

"Could be," replied Ramiro, sliding the canoe in among the branches.

The water was lower than it had been the day before. Carmenza saw the great pallid body lying just under the surface, and thought for a dreadful moment that Omacha might be dead. But he lifted his head to breathe, and to look.

"I'm sure his colour is fading," said Carmenza. "He was a much stronger pink.

But look, his mouth is better . . . maybe he could eat. Let's try giving him the fish you caught."

Feeling safer in trousers and boots, Carmenza held on to an overhead bough and hoisted herself into the water. She took two small fish from Ramiro, who began to spread the net. Omar's boots flooded immediately, but the thick soles allowed her to move around more freely than her sloppy sandals had.

Omacha didn't show any fear when Carmenza approached his head. She held a fish underwater, close to his mouth, but before he had a chance to react, the fish revived and darted off. She gripped the second one firmly by the tail, talking to Omacha and telling him to open his mouth. When he did open wide, Carmenza was so surprised and so horrified by the enormously long rows of teeth, that she dropped the fish by mistake . . . straight in.

"He ate it, he ate it!" she spluttered incredulously to Ramiro. "Give me the others."

The dolphin hadn't eaten for over a week, and his mouth hardly hurt. He swallowed the remaining fish in three snaps, lifting his head to receive each one. Carmenza was beside herself with delight.

"We must get some more – he's starving, look how his ribs stick out . . . "

"Come on," interrupted Ramiro, who couldn't help remembering how she had criticised him for wasting time fishing. "Help me get this net right round, otherwise it won't make any difference how much he eats."

Ramiro had already tied one end of the net to a tree on the bank, and draped it along Omacha's left side to one of the saplings near his tail. He took a deep breath and ducked underwater, looping the mesh around a root as deep in the mud as he could reach. Then they stretched it across to the other sapling and pulled it back towards the bank. All this time Omacha never tried to move out of his pen.

Carmenza stepped back to admire their handiwork and overbalanced – she reached out to steady herself on what turned out to be a rotten branch. It gave way with a soggy scrunch, sending her reeling into the water. She came up to a tempest of buzzing and Ramiro shouting:

"Stay down, stay down!"

Carmenza flung herself farther out. She held her breath until she was dizzy, then rose sneezing and sputtering to hear a furious Ramiro telling her what a clumsy fool she was. He changed tone as soon as he saw her. "You've been stung – your face."

The left cheek was swelling up by the second, giving Carmenza a curiously lop-sided, one-eyed look. But the bees had flown off to find a new home.

Omacha appeared uninterested in the

turmoil. He kept up his regular "pfo" breathing sound while they finished the enclosure, running their fingers around the bottom of the net to make sure there were no loose folds or gaps.

Then they stopped and looked at each other. Both had been dreading this moment – they'd kept busy and chatted on about all sorts of details in order to put it off. Ramiro took the stick Omar had given him from the canoe.

"You hold him. I'll try and get it out." He paused. "First we must see whether it'll work."

Carmenza stood by Omacha's head, fully aware that she was in range of a mouth that might look as if it was smiling, but contained more teeth than she'd imagined possible. She put her hands on the dolphin's back, behind the blow-hole. Ramiro, on the other side, stroked Omacha and felt carefully under the in-jured flipper. Yes, he sighed with relief,

there was a small barb sticking through. Now he felt for the little hole at the base of the spike into which the harpoon shaft fitted, and cut off the last few centimetres of the cord.

Taking his time, Ramiro braced himself as steadily as he could on the slimy bottom, wiggled the smoothly polished stick into the harpoon head with one hand, held the flipper firmly with the other, and pushed with all his strength.

Omacha's body arched clear of the water, his tail thumped violently, and his head crashed from side to side. Carmenza fell under him. Unable to see anything, she scrabbled desperately to pull herself free, then felt Ramiro's welcome tugging on her leg. But Omar's loose boot came off in his hands, and finally it was Omacha's own sideways nudge that rescued her.

"D-did it come out?" she gulped.

"I don't know, I don't even know where that stick is – there's blood in the water."

Omacha was calm again, despite the agonising treatment. Ramiro bent over the flipper, afraid that the dolphin would lash out to prevent him touching it. He found the end of the stick piercing right through the flipper, flush against the flank.

"It's out, the spike's out!" he said triumphantly. "Now for that stick."

This was easy – Omacha barely flinched as Ramiro pulled it clear, though he let out a brief squeaky-squawk.

"Omar was right, and he hadn't even seen it," said Carmenza.

"He usually is right – and he had seen it in a way." Ramiro didn't try to explain Omar's dreaming, but Carmenza half understood, and for once didn't feel he was being deliberately mysterious.

"Is Omacha suffering? What does he think? You can't tell anything from looking at him . . ." Carmenza's voice trailed off.

"I'll go and catch some more fish,"

94

said Ramiro at last, wading over to the canoe.

Carmenza stroked Omacha gently on his back, then along his snout. He lifted his head out of the water and nuzzled against her hand in a trusting sort of way. She felt she was comforting him.

Before Ramiro returned, and before it sank too far into the mud, she wanted to find the harpoon spike. She swished the water away from the dolphin, so there wouldn't be any blood close to him, but his wound was still bleeding. It wasn't pleasant searching for the spike with her head underwater; she groped methodically through the mud and roots under Omacha's right flank until her fingers touched the iron head.

It was too big and sharp to hide in her pockets; Carmenza tucked it into the cleft of a tree on the bank and sat down near Omacha to wait. The forest noises seemed less familiar now that Ramiro wasn't with her – creaks, whistles, screeches, zings and trills mingled with the distant donkey-like braying of the screamer bird. She was wet and chilly in the deep, dark-green shade, and wherever she moved ants swarmed over her.

Omacha was obviously aware of her. Twice he made a squeaky chirruping sound in response to her humming. He lifted his head occasionally, and flexed his body, but Carmenza kept ordering him to stay still so his flipper would heal more quickly. She was confident that he would soon be eating a large meal. When Ramiro returned with the fish, and Omacha refused to open his mouth, it was a terrible disappointment.

"But why, if he ate before? Is he hurting so badly?" she wailed.

Ramiro was busy with two pads containing leaves and bark shavings. He smeared them with a yellowy ointment, and told Carmenza to press one on each side of the flipper while he bound them in place, criss-crossing the bandage over Omacha's back and around his other flipper. The result was messy but firm, and Omacha would have difficulty undoing it. He had accepted what must have been very painful handling without a struggle – just a slight quiver now and then. Omar had explained that the leaves and bark would help fight infection in the wound – their healing power would be released as the water soaked through.

"There's nothing else we can do. Come on – we must get my father to put something on your face, it looks awful," said Ramiro tactlessly.

The fishing spree

Omar went out to fish at dusk. He had sent Ramiro and Carmenza back to Sacha Yacu during the afternoon, having promised to feed Omacha himself.

A pair of scarlet and blue macaws soared high across the water calling noisily in their harsh, grating voices as they flew into the forest. On the opposite side of the lake, terns swooped and squabbled while a fishing hawk watched from above. Among the splashing birds Omar saw first one and then two Inia dolphins. He paddled over to join the fishing spree.

The terns flew off when he approached, but the dolphins remained. One was grey, with a large pregnant belly, the other a blotchy pink and grey mix. Omar whistled, and the dolphins came up behind the canoe, huffing loudly. He drifted on towards the bushes growing on the mud-bank at the edge of the lake. The dolphins suddenly whooshed forward on either side of the canoe, and a mass of silvery fish flashed ahead, caught between Omar and the bank. He threw his spear again and again and again, piling fish on fish in the bottom of the canoe.

Driven by the dolphins, the fish returned once more. Omar chose carefully, spearing those small enough to be swallowed whole by Omacha, and it didn't take long to catch enough for a hungry dolphin. The moon came and went behind scudding clouds as Omar paddled down the lake, the grey female Inia following him.

A little moonlight filtered through the trees into Omacha's forest den. Omar checked that the bandage was still on, and offered Omacha a wriggling fish. His mouth opened greedily. One after another, more than twenty fish disappeared down the pink gullet.

Omar ran his hand along Omacha's snout, and around the inside of the mouth. The back teeth were worn down and chipped after many years of chewing, the front ones felt sharp. He touched the gash on the upper jaw very gently. When he took his hand away, there was a tooth lying in his palm. Silently, he thanked Omacha for the gift.

The canoe floated among the branches while Omar went into the forest. He was gone for an hour, and he returned without the tooth: he had hidden it carefully, so it should not be a danger to anyone.

The grey female stayed near her mate when Omar left. She swam in closer and pulled at the net, but did not tear it. Nor did Omacha try to free himself. Though his wound was already less painful, he could not turn nor balance properly. He would be in danger out in the deep open water, especially from speed boats, fishing nets – or men with harpoons. His mate, now so close to giving birth, was less anguished than before, for she knew he could breathe and eat. He moved nearer the net, and she rubbed against him. She kept Omacha company through the night.

Low water

Ramiro, Carmenza and Manuel had never hated the hours they spent shut up in school as much as they did that week. All three were impatient, inattentive and difficult, and their moods affected everyone in the classroom, including the teacher, who was finding the rainless hot days terribly trying.

Manuel wanted to be away in the forest plucking birds from their nests and making himself useful to Pablo and Roberto. He was missing out, sitting at his desk, and by mid-week he couldn't stand it any longer. He didn't go to school on Thursday. This was an enormous relief to Carmenza – she had become the main target for all his frustration. He had stolen her colour pencils, put a poisonous frog in her lap and teased her non-stop about her secretive talks with Ramiro. What Carmenza didn't know was that he'd also picked up a few tantalising snippets about Omacha.

Carmenza and Ramiro discussed every detail of the dolphin's progress, relying on sketchy messages sent by Omar when Ramiro's mother went out to work in the garden. The patient was doing well, she said, but there might be a new problem: Omar himself was only eating certain foods, and seemed preoccupied. It was infuriatingly vague, and they couldn't get all the way out to the lake after school – Ramiro because his class stayed later, and Carmenza because of her radio job.

They weren't the only ones feeling disgruntled – most of Sacha Yacu's inhabitants were grumbling for one reason or another. The river had fallen too low for the pump, so there was no water in the taps. And the rain-water for drinking had run out. All day, people were toiling up from the river-bank laden with buckets, and though the mayor announced over the loudspeaker that water should be boiled, several children had bad diarrhoea.

Everyone blamed the mayor because the money for the drinking-water plant had run out again. And he couldn't get to Leticia to complain to the authorities – nor could anyone else: a union strike had upset fuel deliveries, which meant there wasn't enough to run the electricity generator for more than one hour a night, and motor boats were drawn up uselessly on the bank. Only Pablo and Roberto seemed to have unlimited petrol locked away in the boathouse, but they were being very mean with it and refusing to sell to anyone.

On top of all this, the vegetation cut down to make new gardens was being burned, and the smoke drifted through

Sacha Yacu, dirtying washing and stinging eyes.

Zoila took Orlando to see the doctor at the health centre. Uninterested and distant in her white coat, she said lots of kids were sick, it was the time of year, and Zoila should be sure to boil the water. But the peculiar thing was that Orlando didn't have diarrhoea or a bad fever, he was just listless, weak and whiny. He was losing weight and lay half asleep in the hammock for hours on end. Carlos, who was as worried as Zoila, accused her of neglecting Orlando and told Carmenza she shouldn't have let him bathe on a breezy evening. Carmenza knew it wasn't her fault, but felt guilty all the same.

The only person who seemed oblivious to the general discontent was Blanca. With starry-eyed selfishness, she spent most of her waking hours wondering how she looked – her hair was now wavy with blond steaks – whether Pablo liked her, and if he would take her off to some exotic big city when he left. There was one advantage in this for Zoila: any housework or cooking for the visitors could be left to Blanca.

Carmenza hadn't given the visitors' activities much thought – her family was doing quite well out of them, and needed the money that poured out of their pockets. Nearly every day Carlos took Pablo and Roberto to other villages in the area, usually by river, sometimes along forest trails. They were buying up all the birds they could lay their hands on, and many other animals too.

Then, on Thursday afternoon, the radio operator gave Carmenza a message for Pablo, and she went to look for him at her aunt's house. No one answered her knocking so she walked through to the back. The yard had been turned into a zoo. Everywhere she looked she saw cages – of birds, monkeys, tiny marmosets, snakes and baby turtles. There were three ocelots and five coatis – Carmenza recognised one of the long-nosed furry coatis as Ana's brother's pet.

At first she was amazed; but the more she saw the more disgusted she grew. The toucans were in a terrible state, bedraggled and cramped. Some of the parakeets lay dead in the bottom of their cage. One ocelot was miserably thin, another was mangey. A few cages sat directly in the scorching sun. Carmenza was used to eating game and seeing forest animals kept as pets – Sacha Yacu was full of them. But somehow the sheer size of this collection made her understand why everyone complained that the hunting was no good any more and that the animals were disappearing.

Suddenly she realised that she'd been lingering far too long, and should be back at the radio. But those poor toucans

. . . Before Carmenza had time to regret it, she undid the bamboo cage and let down one side. The birds perched on the edge waving their huge yellow and black bills, then tried stretching their wings. Without waiting to see them take off, she flew through the house and down the path, only to bump into Pablo as he arrived.

"Someone's calling you from Leticia at half past four," blurted Carmenza in confusion.

"Right, I'll be there . . . what a whirl-wind!" he laughed as she dashed off. Half-way back she ran into her Uncle Juan, who seized her arm and refused to listen when she said she was needed at the radio.

"What are you up to with that net, that's what I want to know? I happened to ask Carlos when he planned to return the harpoon, and he says, what about the net? You're lucky I didn't give you away."

Carmenza squirmed. "Don't tell about

the net, and I promise I'll bring the harpoon on Saturday."

"Make it tomorrow – the water's low,
and I want to catch a pirarucú before the
season ends."

She didn't know how she was going to
retrieve the spike from the lake so soon.
To make matters worse, the radio was
much busier then usual – people couldn't
travel, so they called instead. The operator
was furious that she'd delayed, and said
that if Carmenza was so unreliable, it
wouldn't be difficult to find a replace-
ment. Carmenza sulked at the unfairness
of it – the one thing she took seriously in
life was her job.

All through the hot afternoon she ran
hither and thither with messages. When
Pablo came in for his call from Leticia,
she was waiting for her next errand in
the crowded room, and sidled close to
the radio to listen to his end of the
conversation.

"We'll be back pretty soon," shouted Pablo, "and you should be satisfied with the cargo. There's this petrol shortage but I think we have enough to finish up and get down the river. Over."

A garbled question came in from the other end.

"I can't hear you properly – if you're asking about the cargo, it's mainly the usual stuff, but we may be able to get some teeth. Over."

More incomprehensible noises came through.

"Yes, I understand, you're very interested, OK, goodbye."

He paused, looking thoughtful.

"Any sign of Manuel today?" he asked Carmenza.

"He didn't come to school," she said. Pablo nodded as if that were no surprise.

For once Carmenza reached home feeling tired and out of sorts. Her mother was too distraught to notice – Orlando was worse.

"I've done everything I can think of – he seems to have lost all his strength. If the doctor doesn't do something tomorrow, I've a good mind to take him to a spirit doctor," she said defiantly.

"Don't be ridiculous!" Carlos flared up. "If the doctor's no good we'll have to go to Leticia, to the hospital."

Carmenza half-listened to the rest of the argument. Zoila's remarks about Orlando's strength were zinging around and around in her head. She stared at Orlando – it was true, he had no spark, not even the energy to cry. It was as though he was fading gradually away. She thought about the harpoon, and Omacha's injury, and knew she had to get out to Omar.

She changed into her jeans and tried to edge out of the house. But Carlos saw her.

"What are you doing, sneaking off to play when your mother needs you?"

All Carmenza's resentment against Carlos boiled up.

"And you?" she shouted. "Haven't you realised it's all your fault?"

She pelted up the hill to find Ramiro. The first thing he said was: "Manuel knows."

Carmenza was appalled. "You mean about Omacha?"

"Of course – what else?" said Ramiro, puzzled.

She hesitated, ashamed of what Carlos had done, and reluctant to tell Ramiro that her stepfather was responsible for the harpooning. But maybe he knew any-way . . . and for Orlando's sake she had to explain why she must see Omar.

Ramiro understood, and suddenly Carmenza realised he wasn't stuck-up at all, he was quiet and thoughtful.

"Do you want to go now?" he asked. "It's nearly dark."

"It's not just Orlando. It's Omacha

too. I heard Pablo talking about getting some teeth . . . and Manuel's working with them. Supposing they go to the lake tomorrow . . . Does Manuel know where Omacha is?"

"No, but I think he's got a rough idea. My mother gave something away, and he's so sharp, he put it all together." Ramiro was infected by Carmenza's anxiety. "Yes, we'd better go – but what'll you say to your mother?"

"She's in a state about Orlando – and I fought with Carlos. Let's hope they just think I'm in a big sulk." She grinned. It didn't sound very convincing, but she certainly wasn't going home to beg permission. Ramiro told one of his sisters where they were going, just in case.

They paddled furiously and it was a still night so they made fast progress at first. Carmenza was surprised how well she could see by the tiny sliver of moon and a sky full of stars.

But the long dark channel between the lakes seemed endless. The shadowy trees, so welcome in the daytime, leaned heavily over the water, and the night sounds of the forest closed in on them. Every time a fish jumped Carmenza imagined it was an anaconda snake stalking the canoe. Once, when they heard splashing ahead, Ramiro switched his torch on and it shone into a pair of red eyes.

"Caiman," he whispered.

The water had dropped well down the bank at Omar's garden. They climbed up quickly and went through the trees, Ramiro light-footed, Carmenza tripping over roots and shying away from stray twigs that brushed against her in the dark.

Omar was so slow to respond that Ramiro thought he must be ill. He had a large mosquito net hanging in the shelter now, and all three of them sat inside it while Carmenza described Orlando's sickness and their fears for Omacha.

"I've been fasting, and I have to rest a great deal," said Omar. "I may have neglected Omacha a little – you must go and see him and feed him before you go back. The harpoon wound is not infected and will heal. As long as Omacha is looked after, Orlando will be all right. Carlos did a terrible thing, whether he knew it or not."

Ramiro would have had difficulty finding Omacha's forest den but for the splashing they heard coming from it. And the moment they slipped through the vines, they knew that something dreadful – something they should all have foreseen – had happened.

Omacha was no longer floating in the water.

He lay awkwardly on the mud, his snout snarled in the nylon mesh, his head resting on a fan of roots. The torchlight showed there was just enough water to cover his tail and his flippers, and this had saved him. Every few minutes he thrashed his tail, sending a great shower of spray over his body.

Carmenza knelt down in the mud by his head and stroked and patted him, half-crying with anguish.

"It was the net," she said, freeing his snout. "If the net hadn't been there, you could have swum away before the water got too low! Oh, Omacha!"

Ramiro had already gone to catch some fish. Carmenza stumbled about in the dark, swishing water over Omacha's head and back, thanking the stars that at least he had been in the shade. Only after she had been talking to him, soothing him and bathing him for several minutes did she undo the bandage. The criss-crosses of cloth had actually helped keep Omacha's back moist, because they were soaked by his tail splashing. She felt rather than saw that the wound was nastily ragged, but there seemed to be no swelling and

Omacha barely reacted to her touch. She tugged the bandage free and spread it all over his back and head, leaving the blow-hole uncovered. The arrangement was not unlike the wet sheets which the foreigners had used to protect the dolphins they'd caught for the zoo.

The hide-out was like a dark, slimy cave, alive with twittering bats. To keep away her own fears, Carmenza went on talking to Omacha while she cleared logs and branches, trying to make him more comfortable. Then she began to untie the net, which was so entangled that it was a miracle it hadn't torn. Swarms of insects were attacking her arms and neck, she had already lost one sandal deep in the mire, and she was floundering blindly in a hopeless mess when Ramiro's torch beam at last glittered through the leaves.

"I'm sure a dolphin helped me," he said. "I heard one breathing, and then the fish were being driven towards the canoe."

He gave some fishes to Carmenza and took a handful himself. Omacha opened his mouth, clearly hungry, and Carmenza put one on his tongue. But something was wrong. The dolphin bent his neck as far as he could, and nodded his head this way and that. Ramiro dangled another fish by Omacha's snout; he nodded again, then opened his mouth, and they saw that the first fish hadn't gone down.

"I don't think he can swallow," said Carmenza miserably. "Maybe it's because he's lying in such an uncomfortable position, out of the water. What shall we do?"

"We must try and pull him into the lake," said Ramiro. He shone the torch over Omacha to work out the best way of moving him. The dolphin was lying parallel to the bank, with his injured right side towards the lake and two trees between him and the water. What they had to do was obvious: first he must be turned, and then pulled down between the saplings.

They could see that dragging him round by the tail, even if it could be done, would scrape his belly on the roots. So they stood on either side of Omacha's great body, put their hands underneath him behind the flippers, and tried to lift. At the same time the dolphin made a huge effort to free himself from the mud. But it was no good. He weighed over three hundred pounds, and what had been a natural pen when the water was high had become a perfect trap when it was low.

"I know, let's use the bandage. We can get it underneath Omacha and then drag him without grazing his skin," said Carmenza.

They got to work immediately, pulling the cloth under his tail-flukes. There was nothing wrong with the idea – if only the material had been stronger and Omacha less firmly wedged among the roots.

One on either side of him, Ramiro and Carmenza see-sawed the cloth back and forth, inching it along under his body. The bandage had disintegrated into a tattered rag even before they reached Omacha's belly, with the most difficult part still to go.

Carmenza slumped dispiritedly in the mud and Ramiro's dimming torchlight went out.

Wearily, they splashed some more water over Omacha, wished him a sad goodnight, and paddled back to Omar.

The second journey

Omar dreamed. He wanted to find out whether the rivers were alive and well, and whether the waters were rising or falling. He started on his long journey to the head-waters in a small canoe. It was slow for an old man, paddling against the strong currents. But then two dolphins appeared on either side of him, so he sent them on his mission.

Despite the turbid water, in his dream he could watch them swimming up the River Amazon, neither stopping to feed where streams flowed in, nor playing in the sucking whirlpools. They avoided bobbing tree-trunks and big fishing boats setting their nets. Time passed, and thousands of giant catfish and turtles and piranhas and eels and stingrays swam by. Now the river was narrow, the water shallow. The trees on the bank had all been cut down, and the fertiliser and chemicals used by farmers on their land were filtering into the streams. It was a dreary lifeless place with nowhere for the otters to nest, no healthy fish for them to eat. Then on again. The water tasted foul and the dolphins began to breathe with a horrible rasping sound, their blow-holes clogged by oil which had spilled into the river.

Omar saw this was a dead-end. He whistled to the dolphins and they turned back, swimming fast until they reached the lake. He sent them up a stream that flowed into the lake near his garden. At first it was small and cramped for the dolphins, but as they went on it broadened and grew deeper. The dolphins passed a manatee browsing quietly in a floating field of grass, and when Omar saw that, he was satisfied. Farther up it had rained and the rising water would soon fill the lake again.

Omar heard someone call him and woke to find Ramiro and Carmenza standing outside the mosquito net.

"The rain is coming and Omacha will be all right," he said. "Go home quickly and sleep."

They were already on their way when he called Carmenza back.

"Take this, and make sure it goes to the right person." She felt the cold harpoon head in her hands but was too tired to be surprised that Omar had found it.

Thunder

While Carmenza and Ramiro fell asleep at their school desks, Manuel took another morning off. Pablo had promised him a beautiful hunting knife if he brought in some scarlet macaws – Manuel had bargained hard for the knife because he'd heard Pablo and Roberto discussing the prices paid for macaws in northern countries, and knew they were worth a great deal of money.

During the week he had been spying on a group of macaws up the Sacha Yacu river. He thought he had found two nests with young in them – they were high up near the tops of old tree-trunks, very difficult to reach. He wanted to check them out, and if he couldn't get up there on his own, he'd have to show Pablo. Manuel had seen Pablo shoot small pellets into the wings of large birds, disabling them so they couldn't fly properly and were easily captured. Once the parents had been caught, Pablo could get somebody to cut down the trees and hope the nestlings survived the crash.

Very early, Manuel took Ramiro's canoe upstream, then walked into the forest along an old trail leading towards the lake. He had often trapped birds, taken their eggs and killed them for their feathers or the cooking pot. Stalking them, he'd learned their habits, their calls and their nesting-places. To begin with, Omar had tried to teach Manuel to take only what the family needed from the forest, but he grew exasperated by his youngest son's greed and disobedience. In the end his disappointment was such that he rarely took any interest in Manuel's doings.

Hardly disturbing a lizard, Manuel slipped among fat buttressed trees and straight trunks bound in twisting lianas. The forest floor was drier than usual, but still slightly spongey, and teeming with noisy insects. He waded through a sludgy, reddish stream bridged by a log which had rotted through and collapsed. Soon after, he came to a long-abandoned garden with young umbrella trees competing against each other to reach up for the sunlight. At the edge of the clearing, which had once been farmed by Omar and his family, was a great monster of a tree wreathed in creepers. The ancient tree had always been a landmark and meeting-place when they went to work in the garden. Beside it, much lower but still poking above the new growth, stood a prickly palm trunk. Manuel was determined to get high enough up the big tree to see the top of the trunk; recently he'd watched macaws landing there, and was sure it held a nest.

He tied his machete to a belt loop on

his shorts, took off his rubber boots, and started up with the help of the creepers. A raucous alarm call from the canopy confirmed that he'd probably guessed right. He leaned out to make sure there were no ants' or bees' nests above him and struggled up towards a cluster of orchids growing in a cleft.

Just as he reached for a hand-hold beside the plants, an emerald-green snake's head sprang out. Manuel very nearly fell in his desperate haste to get as far away from that poisonous head as possible. He half slid, half scrambled down, and was going so fast by the time he hit the ground that he pulled away a whole section of creeper, and a host of nasty creatures came cascading down on to him.

Perhaps it wasn't such a good idea after all – he'd been lucky not to land on his machete blade. Then he noticed a perfectly round knot-hole, which had been covered by the creeper. Ever curious, he jabbed a stick into it, and felt a small empty hollow – or so he thought, until he risked his finger and it touched something inside. Manuel hooked the something out with care and found a tooth in his hand. It obviously wasn't a jaguar tooth – he'd seen plenty of those. The only other kind of tooth anyone would hide was a dolphin's. That was it! Manuel couldn't believe his discovery. All this mystery about some dolphin near the garden, and Ramiro and Carmenza suddenly so pally, it must have a connection with the tooth. Probably he only had to go on walking to the lake and he'd find the dolphin.

Or, better still, he'd show the tooth to Pablo and they'd search the lakeside in his boat. He pulled on his boots and picked up the loosely woven basket he'd brought in the hope of trapping a bird.

Barely two paces away there was a small red bundle of feathers flailing among the leaves. This was incredible!

The dolphin tooth had worked already, thought Manuel jubilantly as he put the panic-stricken red and blue macaw in his basket. Perhaps it had tried to fly off when he descended so noisily down the tree – but the wings weren't strong enough to carry it away, only to soften its fall.

Manuel was so eager to find Pablo that he practically ran back to the canoe. All the way down to Sacha Yacu he was gloating at the thought of Ramiro and Carmenza stuck in the oven-like classroom while he'd been unlocking their secrets.

Sacha Yacu was hotter than ever. Some people said the climate was changing because of the holes in the ozone layer of the atmosphere, and others nodded wisely at such comments, forgetting that they complained about the climate every year – sometimes there was too much rain, sometimes too little. The sun's rays were burning and needle-like, and waves of heat flowed back out of the earth. Far away it was thundering again.

Manuel found Pablo dozing on his bed. Excitedly, he thrust the basket at him.

"What's the good of that?" said Pablo crossly. "It's dead." The fledgling was already going cold – its rough descent from the nest had been too traumatic.

"Oh . . . but there are more," said Manuel, undismayed. "And I'm sure I know where the dolphin is now – let's go out to the lake."

Pablo played with the tooth, interested. "OK, we'll try the lake, but it'll have to be tomorrow. I want to go up to another village this afternoon, they're supposed to have some stuff waiting for us to collect. D'you want to come?"

Manuel hesitated. A ride in the speedboat was attractive . . . but so was the hunting knife, and he hadn't earned it yet.

"I've got other nests to look at," he said.

Pablo shrugged. "Well, I'll hang on to this, and see if it brings me something special." He winked and put the tooth in his button-down shirt pocket. "What else?" he asked Manuel, who was still hanging around.

"I just wanted to know . . . well, how do you get the birds out of the country?"

"Thinking of going into the business yourself, are you?" laughed Pablo. "We're not involved in that – we hand all the animals over to an American and he hides them in boats going down the Amazon, or sometimes he'll send a whole planeload out by night. A lot die on the way – I think he just packs them in and hopes for the best – but he blames us. So make sure you get healthy birds! And do the cages up properly, I don't want to lose any more because of your carelessness. Toucans fetch a high price!" Although Manuel had insisted he always fastened the cages when he fed the animals, Pablo seemed to think the loss of the toucans was his fault.

The rumbles of thunder were getting stronger and the heat denser as Manuel went down to the river. He was sidetracked into playing volleyball by a group of friends who'd just come out of school. Carmenza saw him on her way home, and hoped he was concentrating too hard on the game to notice her – but he glanced up.

"You don't know what I know," he sang out. "And I know all your silly secrets." He grinned and bared his teeth, running a finger around his mouth.

Carmenza didn't feel she could cope with Manuel on her own, so she decided to forget him until Ramiro finished school. She had her own immediate problem, which was how to swap the fishing net for the harpoon without raising Carlos's suspicions.

Nobody was home. Carmenza pulled

the net out from under the bed she shared with Blanca, removed the twigs and leaves from the mesh, and rolled it up as neatly as possible. It was still damp, but she put it in the sun by the door, as if her uncle had just dumped it there.

Next she took the harpoon head out of one of her best shoes, collected the long pole from its place behind the front door, and hurried out.

Zoila was on her way in, carrying Orlando.

"Where are you off to with that?" she asked. "And we haven't talked about last night's behaviour either – come right back inside with me."

Carmenza sighed, replaced the shaft, and sat at the table watching her mother settle a whimpering Orlando in the hammock.

"What have you got in your hand?" Zoila uncoiled Carmenza's fingers, exposing the iron spike.

"I was just taking the harpoon back – Uncle Juan mended the net, it's outside."

"So I saw." Zoila looked at her oddly. "Have you forgotten that the spike ended up in a pirarucú?"

Carmenza didn't know what to say. Her mother would only think she was getting at Carlos.

"I found it."

"Yes, but where?" demanded Zoila.

So Carmenza told her.

Zoila sat quiet, looking at Orlando.

"It's his spirit. Orlando won't get well until the dolphins give back his spirit," said Zoila. "I took him up to the health post again. The doctor had an emergency, a difficult birth. I like the nurse better anyway – she's lived here much longer and understands our ways, as well as the illnesses you get in this kind of place. Well . . . she thinks Orlando has hookworm – it's a worm that gets in through bare feet, and of course now he's started walking around. But she seemed surprised that he's quite so listless." Zoila showed Carmenza a packet of pills. "He's already had one of these, they're supposed to be very strong."

"Why not take him to Omar," suggested Carmenza. "I've told him that Orlando's sick."

Her mother cheered up at once. "I wanted to see a spirit doctor but Carlos wouldn't hear of it. If he knew what he'd done, harpooning the dolphin!" Zoila shook her head at Carmenza, who was restless to be off. "You haven't even had a bite or a drink. We'll go as soon as you're through at the radio room. Don't say anything to Carlos."

Carmenza nodded. "I'll find Ramiro, he'll come with us."

"And don't fret about the harpoon – I can deal with that," said Zoila. "Eat this when you're sitting around." She gave Carmenza a slice of bright orange papaya.

Carmenza was indignant. "I never sit around!"

During the afternoon clouds began to creep across the sky. Women filling their buckets from the river gazed expectantly upwards, discussing what time the rain would start and how heavy it would be. Rarely had Sacha Yacu been without even a shower for so long.

Carmenza went backwards and forwards to the mayor's office with messages about spare parts for the pump, when the priest would be able to travel, and why the video-tapes hadn't been returned. Don Miguel's suppliers called in saying it wasn't their fault his merchandise was rotting in a Leticia warehouse, with no boats to ship it up to Sacha Yacu. This set the waiting callers to gossiping about how much money he made by charging them ridiculous prices, and how they'd be the ones to suffer, with no sugar or potatoes or powdered milk in the shop. Carmenza had heard it all so many times; absorbed in worries about Orlando and Omacha, she shut off the complaining chatter.

Half an hour before closing time the radio channels packed up; there was too much interference. Carmenza was released in time to meet Ramiro leaving school.

He looked towards the River Amazon and the long bank of black cloud that was rolling over it to Sacha Yacu.

"Omacha will be swimming soon. I'll change and see you by the river." He hadn't even questioned the need to take Orlando out to the lake, thought Carmenza. He must have realised what had happened well before she did, yet he never said anything. She couldn't decide whether this was in his favour or not.

Carlos was ranting around the kitchen like a snarling dog, and Zoila was in tears. Carmenza took no notice; she was too intent on getting Orlando to Omar before the storm broke. The best rain-gear she could find was an old piece of plastic sheeting, which would at least keep him and Zoila dry.

"Come on," she ordered her mother. "We've got to go."

Carlos stood in the door, barring the way out.

"You're not taking my son to a witch doctor, and that's that. Just try, and you'll both be sorry," he said threateningly.

Zoila reached up to the top of the window frame, where she had hidden the harpoon spike.

"If you could tell the difference between a dolphin and a pirarucú, Orlando wouldn't be in this state. Get out of our way!"

Carlos couldn't understand where the spike had come from or what she was talking about. He was genuinely confused, and in his confusion he moved away from the door. Carmenza ran for it, with Zoila close behind carrying Orlando.

They piled into the canoe, Ramiro in the bow, Zoila with Orlando in the middle and Carmenza behind. Ramiro was furious with Manuel, who had "borrowed" his torch without bothering to ask.

It was hard work paddling across the lower lake, with the wind sweeping them sideways and lashing up the waves. The world had turned a heavy, leaden grey, shot through by great zig-zag flashes and scary thunderclaps. Even the forest had lost its brilliance and become a gloomy grey-green mass. Trees cracked and groaned on either side of the channel, anticipating the storm.

The far side of the big lake was shrouded in dust clouds blown off the dry beaches. Heads down, Ramiro and Carmenza put all their strength into staying ahead of the solid curtain of rain driving across the forest. They could see it and hear it long before the first large drops fell on them. Zoila

G.

wrapped herself and Orlando up in plastic, shivering with cold.

Once the rain hit, they bent low to protect their eyes from its force and paddled blindly on. It stung their necks and arms and legs, but they were close to the garden now, and Carmenza and Ramiro imagined the water lapping around Omacha's flanks.

The spirit

Omacha was free. Just a little water, and he had strained to launch his big body out of the mire in which it had lain straddled for nearly two days. He floated. All the agony, anxiety and fear of death flowed out of him. He swam, carefully and painfully at first, but more confidently once he found he could use his injured flipper. He rolled and dived and exulted in being afloat again.

His mate pushed at his belly with her snout, and he took her flipper gently in his mouth. They swam together, surfaced together, breathed together, and let the rain pour down on their backs. Then they fished, because they were both hungry and needed to eat well.

Above the water, the storm swept the

lake. It tore at Omar's shelter, where Orlando huddled in Zoila's arms and Carmenza and Ramiro squidged the mud through their toes. The light was so strange, it might have been a dark day or a moonless night. One moment everything was alight, the next it was black, and then purple and yellow.

Omar chanted, but the noise of thunder drowned his songs until the worst of the storm faded across the forest. He took Orlando from Zoila and laid him on the floor and sat beside him. The baby seemed to be asleep, and finally all but Omar dozed, tired by their journey, lulled by the monotonous beat of the rain.

Rocking back and forth, Omar drew on his pipe and blew tobacco smoke over Orlando. The pipe was of polished wood, with a hollow monkey's bone for the stem. After a time he stopped smoking and sang again, a soft whistling tune. He sang to the dolphins, telling them

Omacha was healed, and it was their turn to come from the water world, bringing back Orlando's spirit.

Carmenza listened drowsily to Omar, and though she understood little of the Ticuna language, she picked out Omacha's name. Through the drumming rain and croaking frogs she thought she heard a dolphin's squeaky call.

An accident

Carmenza awoke, aching and uncomfortable, to a soggy drizzle and the smell of woodsmoke. Omar had lit the fire to dry them out and keep them warm through the chilly night, and now he had a small pot simmering on it. Zoila and Orlando still slept.

"Ramiro went fishing," said Omar. "You must be hungry."

"Am I!" nodded Carmenza emphatically. "What's that? On the fire?"

"It's for Orlando – he's very weak and anaemic. It'll help restore his appetite."

"How do we know if he's got his spirit back?" asked Carmenza, hoping it wasn't a rude question. "I mean, he will be all right, won't he?"

Omar laughed at her embarrassment and shook his head as if she'd got it all wrong.

"I've spent all my life learning, and I still don't *know*. But I believe in the plants and animals, and in the sky and the earth and the water, and I listen to them and try to understand what they can teach me. You helped keep Omacha's spirit alive, and you cared for him."

"Well . . . we took the spike out, and put your medicine on his flipper," said Carmenza, knowing that wasn't really all they'd done or what Omar meant.

Omar cocked his head on one side. "Oh no, it was much, much more – didn't you talk to him, think about him and share his pain? With the help of the forest and the rivers, and all the creatures in them, that's what I can do for Orlando." Omar took the pot off the fire. "The doctor's pills do their work too."

Ramiro came through the misty garden with three gutted fish slung on a stalk.

"They're not biting," he apologised.

"The rain and the cold," said Omar. "But there's enough to warm our stomachs."

Ramiro squatted by Omar in exactly the same position as his father and put the fish on a metal grill over the fire. The bond between the two was so strong that for a moment Carmenza felt as if they lived in a different world.

They all ate fish, and Zoila gave Orlando some of Omar's potion to drink – he obviously didn't like it, but it was good to see him wriggling energetically to express his disgust.

"Shouldn't we make sure Omacha's gone?" suggested Carmenza.

Ramiro and Omar glanced at each other.

"He won't be there," said Ramiro, "but we can go if you like."

The drizzle had stopped and the garden was steaming as the sun heated the sodden vegetation. They left Zoila talking to Omar, emptied the rain-water out of the canoe and paddled up the lake to the hide-out. The water had risen as high as it had been a week ago when they'd found Omacha. Ramiro was right, of course, but he didn't press the point. They turned back.

"Look!" cried Carmenza in delight. "Omacha!"

The scarred mouth and pink, brown-streaked back were unmistakable. Omacha slid along the surface a few metres away, his head far enough out of the water to show an eye. A grey Inia came up to breathe beside him, and the two dived under the canoe to appear the other side.

"He's incredibly pink," marvelled Carmenza. "Just like he was before."

"The grey dolphin – it could be his mate," said Ramiro. "I think she might have been the one that helped me catch fish for Omacha."

"Do you think he'll remember us?"

Ramiro grinned. "I'll throw him a fish once in a while, and perhaps he'll send me some in the water."

They felt a slight bump against the canoe and Omacha came up again. He did a last, deeper dive, humping his back high out of the water, and vanished into the lake.

"You know," said Carmenza companionably, "if I can get into that backyard when Pablo and Roberto aren't around, I'm going to let all the birds go. I told you about the toucans, didn't I?"

"Yes – wild birds don't live long in cages anyway. Wait till I find out what Manuel's been up to!"

After collecting Zoila and Orlando they paddled back towards the channel. The black glassy lake-water reflected a sky full of fluffy clouds; once in the channel it was hard to tell where the real forest stopped and the mirror began. Carmenza felt she could have been upside-down, or above or below the water, and the world would have been the same whether she was swimming or flying. Three Sotalia broke the reflection, leaping so high that they seemed to be jumping for the trees, and a green and brown kingfisher swooped down from his perch.

"Have you noticed," said Zoila over her shoulder to Carmenza, "that Orlando's taking milk?" Carmenza hadn't, but somehow it didn't surprise her.

"I'll tell Orlando about Omacha when he's bigger," she said.

Zoila chuckled. "He probably won't believe a word ... Do you know the story of how dolphins came to exist?"

"Didn't everything start in the water, and then we all came out on to the land, and the dolphins went back again, or something ... ?"

"I'm not talking about science lessons," said Zoila. "This is a real story, an Indian story, and it's about Caballococha, where my mother was born." She changed to her lilting story voice.

"Long ago, all the people who lived in Caballococha were having a tremendous celebration. It was the coming-of-age ceremony for a Ticuna girl, when she became a woman and all her hair was pulled out. My mother went through that, though hardly anyone does it nowadays. They danced in demon masks, and ate and drank for days.

"They made such a scandal and behaved so badly that an immense flood of water swept over the village and drowned it as a punishment. The people jumped into the water and they all turned into dolphins. They rebuilt the town of Caballococha at the bottom of the lake, with houses and electric light and everything. And some of the dolphins swam off to the Amazon, so now there are dolphin towns up and down all the rivers, where they live just like us."

Carmenza paddled absent-mindedly, lost in dolphin day-dreams and only half aware of the vivid rainbow arcing through the sky and down across the water.

But their lazy content was broken by a commotion on Sacha Yacu's waterfront.

"I'm telling you, I don't know where in the world they are – that's if they're still in this world!" The fisherman crossed himself quickly, and several others followed suit. "All I saw was the boat upside-down in some branches on that island just down the Amazon. It was really smashed up, even the out-board had gone."

"They can't just disappear like that . . . " argued Don Miguel, who'd abandoned his shop to hear the news.

"Of course they can," said the fisherman. "People are always disappearing in the Amazon – electric eels stun them, anacondas drag them down, whale catfish eat them . . . "

"Just a minute." Zoila tugged at Don Miguel's shirt. "What's happened, who are you talking about?"

"Didn't you know? Those two animal smugglers, the men you were looking after," said Don Miguel. "They must have got caught in the storm, and they probably had no idea how unkind the river can be . . . if you're going fast, one big log, and that's that." He drew his finger across his throat.

"Was anyone else in the boat?" asked Ramiro quietly.

"I don't know. Carlos used to go off with them but I saw him carving up the baize on the pool table with his cue last night." Don Miguel suddenly realised why Ramiro looked so peculiar. "Ah – you're worrying about your brother!"

Everyone stopped talking and stared at Ramiro.

"Get along home to your mother, quick," said Zoila.

Ramiro was away, leaving Carmenza thinking of all the times she'd seen Manuel following in Pablo's wake.

What should have been a pleasant homecoming was very glum. But Carlos had to admit that Orlando had colour in his cheeks. The sight of him stumbling around the kitchen clutching at saucepans and baskets did them all good. Zoila hid Omar's anaemia medicine well away so Carlos wouldn't see it.

Blanca sat slumped at the kitchen table, her head cradled in her arms, devastated. She had groaned and cried alternately since she'd heard about the boat accident, and occasionally mumbled Pablo's name into the tablecloth – though in truth it was more her chance of getting out of Sacha Yacu than his fate that she was bewailing.

"It's all right, you can stop all that

row," called Don Miguel cheerfully from the front door. "The Leticia hospital just radioed the doctor here to say they've got Pablo and Roberto. Not in too good shape – bones broken, heads cracked – but they're alive."

"What about Manuel, did the hospital mention him?" asked Carmenza.

"No, nothing," said Don Miguel. "Somebody picked the others up at first light – they were lucky."

"Well, if they're that bad I'll pack up their stuff and have it sent down to Leticia," said Zoila. "But wait – they owe me money for the food and the rent."

"You'd better keep something in exchange then, I don't suppose they'll be back," said Don Miguel. "As a matter of fact I was going to suggest to the mayor that we should confiscate their little hoard of petrol. Pity about the out-board."

While they chewed over the details, Carmenza slipped out. Nobody else seemed to have remembered the animals yet, and she wanted to get to them first – otherwise Carlos would probably say he was entitled to sell them off.

The door to her Aunt Sonia's house was open, and it shouldn't have been. Carmenza tiptoed up the steps. Everything was in a terrible mess – clothes on the floor, bags upturned, nets, plastic bags and tools scattered everywhere.

Rummaging among the debris was Manuel. Relief and fury gave Carmenza the nerve to face up to him in a way she had never dared before. She grabbed the top of his shorts and tried to haul him out of the house, yelling that he was a thief, that his great friend Pablo was a vulture, and that a liar and bully like him didn't deserve Omar for a father or Ramiro for a brother. But Manuel was the stronger, and when he threw her off and went on with his search, she raced to fetch Ramiro.

Nothing his brother did could shock

Ramiro. He told Carmenza to stay in the house and dragged Manuel into the backyard. Carmenza tried to calm a tiny marmoset that had somehow got loose and was jumping from bed to chair to floor. It clung to her hair and pulled at her slides and refused to leave its new refuge.

Ten minutes later Manuel came out looking thoroughly downcast – something Carmenza had never seen before – and muttering something about a knife as he left.

Carmenza went out to the yard.

"So he didn't go with them?"

"No – apparently he wanted to find a baby macaw, because Pablo had promised him a hunting knife," said Ramiro. "He was out all night in that storm, and brought the bird in this morning. He decided they owed him the knife."

Ramiro gazed round the pitiful menagerie. "It's even worse than I imagined."

"I think harpooning a dolphin is just as bad," said Carmenza. "Even if Carlos didn't mean to."

"Huh – those toads would have done the same if they'd had the chance," Ramiro said angrily. "Manuel had got hold of a dolphin tooth, and they were going out to the lake to find Omacha today." Carmenza shuddered.

"Did he keep the tooth?" she asked curiously.

"He gave it to Pablo," said Ramiro with a half smile. "It didn't bring them much luck, did it?"

"I must tell Carlos. He won't be so keen on having a dolphin tooth now," she said. "What with Pablo and Orlando."

She sat down on the back step. Many of the animals were even more miserable than when she'd last seen them.

"Poor things, they weren't even sheltered from the storm. Now what?"

Ramiro looked at the marmoset entwined

in Carmenza's hair. "That one seems to have chosen its new home."

He considered the jumbled cages. "We can just let the wild birds go, like you did the toucans." They opened up two cages of parrots, and several more of parakeets and other small birds. It took a few moments for them to realise they were free, then they were off in a great flurry, leaving at least a dozen pathetic little corpses in the cages.

"Some of the animals are people's pets," said Carmenza. "They can just have them back again. Manuel was supposed to be in charge of feeding. I don't think he bothered much."

"The snakes will have to be let out well away from Sacha Yacu. But the fledglings are the real problem, and those baby ocelots."

"I know!" Carmenza's face beamed with her idea. "What about your father? He can look after them, and they'll get accustomed to the forest and go back when they're big enough."

It was the perfect answer, Ramiro agreed.

"I think we should help – there's a lot of them," went on Carmenza. Some high-pitched chattering from the marmoset distracted her. "It's hungry . . . I could come out at weekends, maybe?"

She looked enquiringly at Ramiro because it all depended on whether or not he wanted to take her.

"Yes . . . we can go together," he confirmed.

"And we'll see Omacha," finished Carmenza.

The calf

The grey female had felt the calf moving inside her for some time, but especially during the terrifying period when Omacha was injured and stranded on the mud. At last, after nearly eleven months of carrying the calf, her body was labouring to give birth.

It was night and she wasn't far from Omar's garden, swimming in a shallow part of the lake. Omacha fished quietly on his own at the entrance to the channel, poking the mud with his snout and snapping up the creatures he surprised into flight.

Another female Inia swam near Omacha's mate, watchful and ready to help. The water and the air were warm and still – a good night for a calf to be born.

With her tail moving constantly, and her body bending back and forth to speed the birth, the grey dolphin swam around and around. She breathed often because she was using so much energy. Sometimes she rolled over, or swam sideways, or upside down, concentrating all her efforts on pushing the calf out. Its tail-flukes came first, folded over after being squashed inside for so long; then its back with a tiny dorsal fin, and the flippers, which sprang out from its small body.

Still circling, the mother gave a last tremendous thrust and squeezed the calf's head free into the lake. Quickly, she pushed him up for air.

The other Inia helped her keep the calf floating near the surface while he took his first breaths. He could already swim, though not strongly, and he stayed very close to his mother, just behind her right flipper.

By dawn he was feeding: his mother's

nipples were hidden underneath inside small slits, and when the calf nudged at one or other, she squirted milk into his mouth. To begin with, he fed several times a day.

Omacha joined his mate and their dark grey calf. They often swam near Omar's garden and answered his whistle when he went fishing. The fishermen from Sacha Yacu who saw Omar paddling across the lake wondered whether it was he who was whistling for the dolphins or they who were calling him to the water world.

All Pan books are available at your local bookshop or newsagent, or can be ordered direct from the publisher. Indicate the number of copies required and fill in the form below.

Send to: **CS Department, Pan Books Ltd., P.O. Box 40, Basingstoke, Hants. RG21 2YT.**

or phone: 0256 469551 (Ansaphone), quoting title, author and Credit Card number.

Please enclose a remittance* to the value of the cover price plus: 60p for the first book plus 30p per copy for each additional book ordered to a maximum charge of £2.40 to cover postage and packing.

*Payment may be made in sterling by UK personal cheque, postal order, sterling draft or international money order, made payable to Pan Books Ltd.

Alternatively by Barclaycard/Access:

Card No. | | | | | | | | | | | | | | | | | | |

Signature:

Applicable only in the UK and Republic of Ireland.

While every effort is made to keep prices low, it is sometimes necessary to increase prices at short notice. Pan Books reserve the right to show on covers and charge new retail prices which may differ from those advertised in the text or elsewhere.

NAME AND ADDRESS IN BLOCK LETTERS PLEASE:

....

Name ————————————————————————————

Address ————————————————————————————

————————————————————————————

————————————————————————————

3/87